S. O. L.

A Light Novel

Max E. Keele

Published by Naraka Press,
A Division of Speed of Light Enterprises
All rights reserved.
ISBN: 0615594247
ISBN-13: 978-0615594248

To the three greatest Thaumaturges
of All Time:

Albert Einstein,
Siddhartha Buddha,
and

Phillip K. Dick

and with special thanks to Ruth,
Truly the light of my life

Contents

-0-

Let There Be Light

It is about time.

A dead man stands poised at the edge of the universe. In the world, he died at the end of the year 1947, but in this place, he has been dead forever. From the brink of the void, he looks down into the world at a fresh, clean page of his own design. His eyes close as he visualizes the art that is to come, the game about to begin. He laughs. What a course his fate has taken! To disdain Death and live to create again. To experience the very source of love itself. To walk strange shadows of the Earth, not as a man, but as Master. Everything is ready.

It is almost time.

-1-

Line Drawing

A straight-edge highway runs diagonally across a blank page, a desert of black and white — no gray. The blacktop line runs clean and sharp in two directions: fore and aft, past and future. The highway's vanishing points punctuate the horizon, period. All four edges of the page terminate in a remote and jagged fringe; the page has been rudely torn on every side. Just on the page at the right, next to the line-highway, rests a microscopic speck, perhaps animate, perhaps only dust.

-2-

Wheels

The old DeSoto rolls through the desert, as quiet and smooth as a bowling ball on velvet. The only sound: faint clicks from a tired air-conditioner and a muffled brrr from the motor. The DeSoto is in incredible shape for all its age: not one crack in the dash, not one speck of rust. It plows through heat waves and mirages with ease. It greets every small bump with liquid determination. Bugs have splattered like dark stars across the heavy chrome bumper and grill.

For all this, the car's paramount feature is the subtle power behind its irresistible grin.

-3-

Redundant Ubiquity

Rupert sleeps. He breathes in parched air and tiny flying insects, breathes out precious moisture and sighs. Under a rock, like a reptile, Ru sleeps. He hides from the refulgent sun of desert morning. He dreams of cool waters and a mountain drenched in green. In his dream, he talks with a sparkling young woman in the center of a sodden field of flowers and wild grass. She wears a pink robe and a pair of silver earrings—cleverly wrought bullwhips, of all things. Her every step is a dance. Her perfume smells of life, or spice perhaps.

Cool water reflects the quivering air.

-4-

Charcoal

Closer now: the speck becomes visible; the texture of the page grows distinct. Tiny lines cross-hatch, disorganized and unruly, and what was a featureless surface has developed bumps, plateaus, shallow depressions. A grayness softens the lines; shadows provoke the illusion of depth.

-5-

The Stripper

The Master watches her walk the length of the stage on her hands with her wire-tight legs held in full splits. The 1812 Overture roars from huge speakers. Church bells ring of victory and the cannonade begins. The stripper's body arches and she falls over backward into a bridge. Unhappy with the timing, she rises, restarts the music, begins anew.

To the Master, she is something more than an amusement, something less than a concern. But when he watches her pull herself from the bridge to her feet with leg muscle alone, not he, not the completely soulless, nor even the long-dead faggot Tchaikovsky will avoid being moved to erection.

When Felicia finishes the 1812 with a lit roman candle stuck to each nipple, neither death nor preference will spare the staid composer indignity; and the Master's toothy grin, will, for one fleet moment, look very much like the front grill of an old DeSoto.

Clearly, it is only a trick of the light.

-6-

Sunrise

Time is morning. Pink daggers stab at a bruised sky.

Ru crawls out from under his rock and stretches, scratches, yawns. He reaches for his copper flute like it was the day's first cigarette.

This is the desert at its coolest: at night the cold air scorches, by day the wind is fire, at dusk the sands are molten. Dawn is cool.

Cool music drifts up to greet the day.

-7-

Pastel

Closer still, the speck becomes a defined shape; it can be seen to possess the quality of motion. Ridges and valleys on the page grow three-dimensional and solid. With proximity it becomes possible to see above the page. A chalky blue merges with several shades of pink to color the sky. Other pale hues spread into the landscape: a rust and ocher tint to the page, a purpling at the ragged borders. The new tones have brought feeling, a taste of warmth, a scent of luminosity.

-8-
Aleis

Aleis is a witch. She makes her martinis with nettle wine instead of vermouth. She draws enigmatic runes on the filters of her cigarettes. When she drives, she burns myrrh in the ashtray. Her eyes tell a tale that much older than seems possible: a sadness interminable, a weariness ancient, an obligation unending. But whether or not she has born an eternity of awesome responsibilities, she is in incredible shape for all that.

The highway flows beneath her car like water under a bridge. She drives up onto the page as if she owned it. She honestly believes that she does. Aleis is an artist. She sings soprano along with the Gregorian chant that echoes from the stereo. She sips a nettle martini from a stemmed crystal glass. Suddenly, the heavy mood shatters. She laughs, excited.

Aleis is going to a party.

-9-

Wisdom

Master:

What's the fun of being God, if nobody genuflects?

GIL:

It passes the time. Your move.

-10-

Watercolor

Close enough now, the shape has taken the form of a man. Colors have deepened, and developed flavor. The rust and ocher page becomes a rocky wasteland strewn with all the shades of color that there are, random and chaotic. At this range, sounds are heard. The love-coos of mourning doves, the shrill twitch of crickets, the bark of a lone toad, the animated bitching of magpies all blend in symphony with the incandescent sunrise. The hollow sweetness of flute music improvises wild jazz riffs that dart and soar and blaze, subdued only by the vastness of the page.

-11-
Meat Parts

Dan the trucking man takes a sloppy gulp from a pint bottle of lime vodka. Green effluvium dribbles down his quivering jowls. A pile of Tootsie Rolls a hundred deep jitters on the seat to his right. He peels one with his teeth and shoves it into his mouth. Brown spittle accents the line of green that drips down his chin and spatters random droplets on his overstuffed tee shirt. Dan belches. He raises one massive ham, farts loudly, and grunts with pleasure. Out of the stench comes a strange dancing sound, like the music of a crowd's embarrassed laughter.

Dan's truck is a thirty-five ton dumper full of meat parts. This seems somehow appropriate.

-12-

Sooner or Later

Rupert sits cross-legged on a faded green blanket, blowing feral melodies through a slim copper flute. He is as wild and naked as his song. Rust colored hair falls tangled to his ocher shoulders. His eyes squint from concentration and glare. They are young eyes, but their color is as worn and faded as the blanket. Spicy sage mingles with the odor of his unwashed body. His music carries the scent of cheap wine, the stink of vile sausages. His blanket smells of sweat and urine.

A two-foot long orange salamander sleeps coiled around Rupert's neck, its tail clenched securely in its mouth. It awakes, blinks amphibious eyes and crawls around to perch on Rupert's shoulder, yawning and stretching.

"Hey," says the salamander. "Cool it, okay? Don't you think it's a bit early for that kind of shit?"

Rupert's melody evaporates into breath. The flute drops to his lap. "Good morning, Py. Sleep well?"

"Just fine, until the concert started," Py snorts. "I was dreaming that you finally decided to settle into society. You had a nice little house, with a garden and a little wading pool. You even had a girlfriend. But just as you were finally about to lose your virginity, some goddamned banshee commenced to wailing, and I woke up. Serves you right."

Rupert hoists the salamander by his tail, looks square into his bulging eyes. "I thought you liked music."

"Good gods, Ru, will you never learn that there's a time and place for everything? Morning's the time for meditation and philosophy, not rock 'n roll."

"That's a crock," Rupert says. "You just like to sleep in."

Py flicks his sticky tongue at Rupert's nose. "As you like it. Now put me down. That's a tail, not a goddamned handle."

Rupert laughs. "Okay, okay. Go catch a fly, or something, while I get dressed. And watch out for newt-eaters. I hear the desert's lousy with them."

"Newts?" Py rolls his eyes, in two different directions. "You know any newts?"

Rupert pulls on a pair of tan canvass pants. His toe catches in a knee-hole, tears it wider, and dust flies from the desiccated fabric. He slips his grimy feet into rotted high-top sneakers. He puts his flute into a burlap potato sack, ties it with a strap, slings it over one shoulder. He hefts his walking stick, a fine length of ash with a smooth, round head, and calls out, "Py! Let's go!"

The amphibian hasn't wandered far. "Bloody rot. Are we walking again? This stinking desert's too damned hot; let's wait for a ride."

"Ride? There hasn't been a car by here since we got let off. You got no right to bitch anyway. I do all the walking; you just sit up there and lecture."

So they set off down the straight-edge highway, Py riding high on Rupert's shoulder, watching for cars and spewing a torrent of good-natured criticism. "Seriously, Ru. I wish you'd at least try to settle in somewhere. I've done my best to educate you; now it's time for you to try it on your own. All this wandering around has really gotten rather pointless, not to mention uncomfortable. I mean, we've seen everything there is to see out here. Salt Lake, Denver, Vegas—we've been there. Yellowstone, Grand Canyon, Coors Brewery, been there, too. We're turning into a couple of common vagrants! Just because you never had a childhood doesn't mean you can get away with being a bum. Childhood's a waste on most folks, anyway. Now if it were just me, I mean, if I was all alone, who could expect any different? After all, I'm just a simple amphibian. But you, you're a bright enough sort. You could be just about anything you like. You should be in college, or working, or in the goddamned army, or something. Don't you ever wonder what it would be like to live in a city, in a house, like everybody else? Don't you ever want to get laid? We haven't slept two nights in the same place since we left Oregon. You must have liked one of the towns we've seen. What was wrong with Colorado Springs? Now there was a place you could get used to. Admit it. You could get some kind of job, find yourself a nice little apartment, maybe with a duck pond, and I could go back to being a lazy, bug eating machine. You might even manage a girl, even. Ru, I'm telling you, it's time you settled down. You've got to join society someday; no way out of it. And you know, I won't always be here to keep you out of trouble. You're like a son to me, Ru, I just can't watch you wander aimlessly for the rest of your life. Damn it, you can't dodge responsibility forever. I'm serious. Look, you could...." Py chatters on for miles, but Rupert doesn't mind; he just strides along, digging the freedom in the late morning air.

A little after noon, Py spots an automobile creeping through the distance toward them. As it emerges from the usual mirage, Rupert extends his thumb.

The car is a dirty blue DeSoto, an antique. It zooms on by, grinning. Py chokes on dust and indignation. "You ignorant newt sucker! You, you frog-eating mother of drought! I hope your tires turn square! I hope your asshole heals over! I, uh, I hope…."

But the DeSoto has stopped. It backs slowly toward them. Rupert laughs. "Now aren't you ashamed of yourself?" He holds open his sack and Py slithers in, contritely. Rupert attempts to straighten his hair, but it proves hopeless.

The passenger door pops open, as if by magic. Rupert climbs in.

-13-

The First Limerick

There was a young man name of Ru,
Who's brain was divided in two.
    He walked through the sands
    Of sun-painted lands,
And dreamed dreams that sometimes came true.

-14-

Party Favors

There is much to do, and so little time. The RSVPs are stacked like cordwood in the corner; everyone is coming. The gala has already begun, yet much remains. There are drugs to collect, punches to brew, hors d'oeuvres to catch, games to conclude, traps to lay, waiters to hire, defenses to prepare, costumes to rent, bands to contract, monoliths to transport, precious metals to transmute, spirits to appease, situations to invent, menus to plan, seatings to arrange, knots to tie, lines to draw, oil to boil, wine to respirate, knives to sharpen, altars to consecrate, needles to sterilize, eggs to hatch, entertainments to create, constructions to construct, rugs to shampoo, crystal to polish, sushi to chill, wars to wage, and favors to wrap. The Anniversary of the Pyramids happens only once in a millennium; nothing can be left to chance.

It is about time.

-15-

Six Obvious Lies

"Get in." Aleis looks over the top of her rose-pink sunglasses. An arcane smile distorts the symmetry of her lips.

"Hey, thanks, I really appreciate this." Rupert settles into the DeSoto's passenger seat, lays the burlap sack on the floor at his feet. His mouth dries up and his heart drops a beat as she shifts into drive. He bites his lip as she adjusts her loose cotton skirt. His blood thickens when, with long painted nails, she plucks an olive from her martini and pops it into her smile. His palms begin to sweat when she works the accelerator with a naked foot.

"There's some gin and another glass in the glove box. Ice and olives on the back seat. Vermouth's that unmarked bottle." Her voice is piquant; she sounds like a peculiar cross between ancient virgin and pre-pubescent pop star. "I assume you can make a martini. Not too dry, please."

Rupert's tongue sticks to the back of his teeth. He pulls it loose and mumbles, "I can manage."

"So, just how do you happen to be way out here? Nearest town with more than one gas station was Vegas, seventy miles ago. You walk all that way?"

"That's funny. It didn't seem that far." Rupert hands her a drink, works on his own. "I guess distance is relative, too."

She sips her martini. "Well, I can take you as far as Needles. I'm really headed for Big Bear Lake, but I've got things to take care of in Needles. Good martini."

Rupert pulls hard at his cocktail. "Hmmm. Wow, tastes good, but a bit sharper than I'm used to."

Aleis laughs. "I make my own vermouth."

They ride for thirteen miles without further conversation, drinking and listening to frightful music. When they approach Needles, Aleis finally speaks. "Listen, you could probably use a shower, and a clean place to sleep. You can stay with me tonight, if you want." She tucks a stray strand of dark blond hair back into its pony-tail.

Rupert blushes beneath the dirt on his face. "Uh, sure. I mean, thanks. I'd like that."

She offers him a cigarette. "Oh, we never introduced ourselves. I'm Aleis."

Rupert is entranced by what appears to be a half-finished pentagram drawn on the cigarette's filter. "I've been told that my father's name was Aleister. But I never met him; he's long dead." He lights up, and smokes quietly, too numb, too drunk to tell more lies.

-16-

War Games

A small armored patrol—four tanks, a half-track and a mobile rocket launcher—rumbles in a snaky line through the desert page. The Master has sent his Marines on armed maneuver around the perimeter. A rusty dust cloud follows them. From the cloud whispers an odd melody, like the murmuring voices of an anxious audience, waiting for the curtain's rise.

In the lead tank, Cooper, Batman and the Sick Lieutenant play a word game, Botticelli, for drugs. Each time a player receives a "no" answer, he must reach blindly into the grab-bag, extract a pill at random, and eat it without looking. The bag contains a sample of every mind-bender known to man. Cooper has not been doing well; his eyes are beginning to freeze over. Batman has been lucky so far; he sits on the edge of an ammunition box, foot tapping a Dexedrine rhythm. The Sick Lieutenant was born to be a junkie; he seems unaffected.

The Master plans his next move. The patrol rumbles on.

-17-

Strange Particles

And so, it happened that in the year 1222 AD, during the course of unrelated experiments, an old alchemist named Albertus Magnus stumbled across a minor miracle. As he stirred a mixture of earth, air, fire and water, he was shocked to see growing there a large, vibrant pink stone. Through random observation he discovered that the rock manifested certain curious properties — most interesting: when placed in proximity to common elements, the stone transmuted them to purest gold. Magnus called it the Philosopher Stone.

Now, one could have expected the alchemist to be quite pleased with his fortune, and surely, for a time, he was. Until a small problem developed: the Stone could not be made to discriminate. Before long, his entire laboratory, half of his home, two of his children, three hapless geese, and a bar wench of disputable morals named Felicity had been rendered, irreversibly, golden. This proved embarrassing for poor Magnus, to say the least. He protected himself with expensive magical charms, but the prospect of surviving alone in a golden world did not overjoy him. It was the fear that finally convinced him that the Universe was not yet ready. He painted the Stone with a mystic screen that was guaranteed to last seven hundred and seventy-seven years, then buried it deep within a druid's circle.

And so it happened that Albertus Magnus lived out the rest of his Earthly life quietly — a richer, but humbler, man.

-18-

More Wisdom

Master:
Games, you realize, are nothing but an opportunity to test the application of will in an arena without consequence.

GIL:
Only time will tell, old man. Roll the dice.

-19-

Boxcars

The dusty DeSoto pulls into a Motel 6 parking lot, grinning and panting like a tired, friendly dog. Aleis steps lightly from the driver's side, then holds to the door for a moment while her legs find the ground. Heat waves ripple the air above the hood. Six cylinders cool, cracking and popping like dice in a tin can.

She returns from the motel office with key swinging like a sixth finger from her hand. Lazy, the DeSoto glides into the sixth stall. Its hot engine shudders to sleep with a sigh.

Six oleanders luxuriate along a path lit by six oriental lanterns. The woman and her disheveled companion carry a six-pack of beer, an assortment of bags and an ash walking stick into room number six.

The DeSoto grins in its sleep; the game has begun to get interesting.

-20-

Magic Fingers

Rupert dreams he is at sea in giant sponge-rubber bathtub. He stretches out, more comfortable than seems real. He tries hard to remember why comfort should surprise him, with no success. The sea maintains a glassy calm; the only motion comes from Rupert's gentle breathing.

Suddenly, from out of nowhere, a gargantuan orange sea monster rears an ugly head. It clenches a quarter the size of a dump truck's tire in its fangs. The quarter drops, and as ripples spread, the sea turns to lime green jelly. The ocean quivers and the bathtub rocks. Rupert abandons ship.

The sea serpent laughs, claps its clawed hands and says, "Man overboard! Ru, I swear you're the only person I know who'd panic because of a vibrating bed. One tiny little earthquake and you'd probably drop straight dead."

Rupert levers himself from the floor. He looks around the room, wild-eyed and confused. He shakes his head cautiously, and sits on the edge of the humming waterbed. "Someday, Py, I'm gonna trade you in on a higher life form. Cockroach, maybe."

The salamander snickers, and jumps into the center of the bed. Thick ripples quiver outward, knocking Rupert back onto the floor. "Sticks and stones." Py climbs up on Rupert's bony knee. "And how do you feel this morning? I bet you're tired." Two grins. "You were up all night; hell, it sounded like two warthogs fighting over a gunny-sack full of cats in here. How's it feel to be a real man?"

A fly lands on Rupert's thigh and begins crawling toward his groin. Py snaps it up with fourteen centimeters of sticky tongue. "Suppose I could get you down from the clouds long enough to draw me a bath? Goddamned motel put their faucets too high."

"Sure, no problem." Rupert closes his hand around Py's middle and walks unsteadily to the bathroom. He starts the water.

"Not so much hot," Py says, anxiously. "I'd rather not poach, if it's all the same to you."

"Picky beggar, aren't you." Rupert drops him into the water from two meters up. "Aleis gone?"

"Dammit! Too hot! She split just after you passed out. Disappointed, no doubt. We did have a nice little chat before she left, though. Seems we used to know each other."

Rupert sits naked on the closed toilet lid. He inspects his penis, which is pleasantly sore and sticky. His pubic hair is stiff and matted. He draws an index finger beneath his nose. The aroma of love spins his head with a hundred images of the night.

"Didn't she leave a note, or a message? Anything?"

Py floats on his back, arms crossed over his chest, eyes closed. "Yeah, she left some stuff in there. Damned if I can tell what she saw in you."

The scents of tropical beaches and sweaty heathen rites rise from Rupert's finger. He sighs, and leans back against the toilet tank. Aleis: chanting monks and sharp martinis, the blue DeSoto and that flowered skirt, dainty callused feet, light and easy laughs, that smooth tanned skin, her blood-red lips and nails, dancer legs and dancing laugh, more martinis, her tiny black panties with the silver crescent moon glowing in the center, the fragrances of gin, nettle, coriander, musk and myrrh. Aleis: pushing over-sized sunglasses up her nose, piloting that old DeSoto like Cleopatra's barge, inviting Rupert to share her bath, stroking him with the towel printed in sixes, combing the tangles from his hair, lifting that flowered skirt and inviting him to share that, too. Rupert savors the memory of her sweat-slick body as it moved above him, arched, tense, vibrating faster than the bed. Her eyes clenched tight, and her tongue darting in and out to the rhythm of their pounding blood. Her rocking waves of spastic orgasm. He remembers her licking sticky glaze from his inner thighs, her eyes half shut and dilated. She purred. Stirred by the images, Rupert's reddened penis mills about like an aimless, skinless snake.

"Hey, Ru. You hung over, or what? Give me a lift out of here and take a nice cold shower while I snag a few bugs. There might be a little of that weisswurst left for you, if it hasn't crawled away yet. C'mon, get moving. Day's half gone. Jesus, give the boy a touch of pussy, and he turns into a goddamned potato."

The shower startles his skin and restores some clarity to his mind. More alert, Rupert tingles with curiosity. A note from Aleis! He rushes from the bathroom, dripping.

Py has cleaned the flies from every sill. He lounges on one elbow, toying with an impressive cockroach. "That sausage smells pretty bad," the salamander says, "just the way you like it." He crushes the roach with his tail.

"Man, I haven't seen you this excited since you first heard about girls. Allie left some stuff for you there on the desk."

Rupert vaults the bed, dances to the desk, and is surprised to find a stack of new clothing: blue jeans, a tee shirt, socks and a pair of green boaters. Under the pile lies a crisp nylon knapsack. Under the knapsack, a Gideon bible rests comfortably. It opens by itself to the Revelations of Saint John the Divine, Chapter Thirteen. Between the pages, he sees a sheet of Motel 6 stationary, white and blank.

As Rupert watches, words the color of Aleis's lips form against the page in perfect Olde English script. As he reads them, Aleis's tart voice whispers in his ear. "SORRY I COULDN'T STAY, THINGS TO DO. PLEASE COME TO MY PARTY, SAT. @ 4:44 PM. JUST FOLLOW THE PIE PLATES WITH PYRAMIDS ON THEM. GO TO BIG BEAR LAKE.... JUST FOLLOW THE PLATES. TILL THEN — ALLIE
P.S. I EXPECT YOU, PY, ALSO. CAN'T WAIT TO TALK SOME MORE ABOUT OLD TIMES....

P.P.S. RUPERT, WHY DO YOU MAKE POOR
PY RIDE IN THAT FILTHY SACK?

Py picks pieces of roach shell from his
teeth. "So," he says, "what does she say? She
mention me?"

"As a matter of fact, she suggests that you
become a vegetarian. People who eat bugs gross
her out." The words fade to pastel pink; Rupert
looks on with skepticism. "And we're invited to
a party."

"Well, then, it's a lucky break she's never
seen you gnawing at one of your disgusting
salamis. Party, huh."

The words have totally disappeared and
one corner of the page begins to smolder. "What,
you don't want to go?"

"Are you kidding? I love people parties. I
get to spend all night dodging spike heels, fat
drunks and hungry cats. It's loads of fun. Have
you any idea how hard it is to get a cocktail
waitress's attention from down here?"

Rupert jumps as the page bursts into
flame. It is completely consumed before it hits

the floor. No smoke, soot or ash marks its passing. "Well," he says, "I'll make you a deal. If we go to Aleis's party, you don't have to ride in the bag anymore. Okay?"

"Sure thing, Ru. Live it up. I do wish you'd give some thought to settling down; it's about bloody time."

"Someday, buddy." Rupert dresses in his new clothes, even though he's still damp in places. He chews stale sausage, and shares a warm beer with Py. He stuffs his old gear and the burlap sack into the garbage, packs his few things into the nylon pack, and shuts the bible. Py climbs onto Rupert's shoulder. Rupert hefts his walking stick, and they head for the door.

As he steps into the sun, Rupert freezes. For as long as he can remember, and as of last night, the stick had a head of smooth, polished ash. Now, it wears the head of the dog-god, Anubis.

"Don't look at me," Py says. "I sure as hell didn't do it. Never touched the damned thing."

Rupert shrugs, walks the short distance from the Motel 6 to Route 66, and offers his thumb to the world.

-21-

Another Limerick

There once was a young man named Ru,

Who's mind was a composite stew.

    The chef was the Earth,

    A cook without mirth,

And odds are, we're in the soup, too.

-22-

Junk

An old automobile lies on its side in a gully. Long wild grasses grow through the windows; soft green mosses cover the north face. There is no glass, no wood, no rubber, no cloth or leather—only hollow, rusted metal and the nests of vermin. The car has been here, abandoned in this moist place, for fifty years. It was left, a shiny new '49, as a burnt offering. Left to decay in peace and serenity. Left to nourish the Earth at its own leisurely pace.

The old DeSoto anticipates resurrection.

-23-

Leather

Ruby stands astride her chopped Norton Commando, gazing wistfully at the cool green Lucerne Valley. She slaps the Barstow dust from her black jacket, and the chains tinkle like wind chimes. She rolls herself a cigarette from a pouch of Bull Durham, lights it with a wooden match. A small family of cattle grazes at the side of the road. She watches a new calf suckle, and sighs a cloud of smoke.

She pats the Norton's gas tank. "Fuck, it's purty out here." She sniffles, tosses the butt of her smoke, spits after it, and wheelies out onto the highway. Her front wheel touches down; the bike rides up and over the edge of an invisible page.

A dark, lanky man with a grinning beard stands beneath a sign that points toward Big

Bear Lake Recreation Area. He tips his hat, and the black hollow of his eyes shines fire.

Ruby flashes past him with a wild whoop. Why not?

-24-

Meat Parts II

"Climb on up here, son. The name's Dan. Make yourself to home, heh, heh. What the hell is that thing? Funniest looking lizard I ever saw. Where the hell ya headed?"

Rupert carefully pushes aside a few Tootsies, and settles in. "Hi," he says. From his shoulder, Py glares at the fat trucker. "He's not a lizard. Salamander."

The truck makes a peculiar lilting noise, like a spattering of applause.

"The hell you say. Looks like a damn lizard. Slimy orange lizard." Dan watches Py closer than he watches the road. "Is it housebroke? Don't bite, does it? What you say yer name was? I'm Dan. Dan, the truckin' man, heh, heh, heh."

"I'm Rupert. Nice to meet you. Dan."

"Sure is. Say, you ain't one of them damn hippies, are you? Where ya say you was headed? I'm pointin' to Smogville; that's Ellay to you. Got me a shit-load of animal fragments. Gonna make dog food. Least I hope so, heh, heh."

"We're just going as far as Big Bear," Rupert says.

Dan tears the wrapper off of a Tootsie Roll, and pops it in his mouth, whole. "Want a Tootsie? Them suckers is all that keeps me alive, these long hauls. Don't know what I'd do without 'em." He belches loudly. "How about a little booze? You a drinkin' man, son? Don't trust nobody what's sober, heh, heh, that's what I say." He passes an unopened pint of lime vodka.

Rupert breaks the seal and takes a long slug. "Good stuff."

"Heh, heh. That's it, son. Couldn't live without it. Least ways, wouldn't much want to. Well, I can't take ya to Big Bear, but I'll drop ya in 'Bernadino. That's sorta close. Say, what the hell ya goin' there for? Ain't nothin' this time of year, 'cept maybe a biker party or two. You one of them damn bikers, son?"

Rupert has another drink, then passes back the bottle. "Well, I am going to a party, but I doubt there'll be many bikers. There was this girl..."

"Girl, huh?" Dan wipes off the pint's neck, takes half in one gulp. Fresh green spots appear on his multi-colored tee shirt. "Heh, heh, Bert, you ol' sonovagun. Rich broad with big tits, I bet. Now me, I like 'em with a little meat on 'em." He hands the vodka to Rupert; it sloshes with an eerie, disembodied chuckle. "Whatchya say we hit Ludlow for a lunch break? I'm so damn hungry I could eat what's in the back, heh, heh. We gotta stop for more booze, anyways. Might as well make the best of it."

"Sure," Rupert says. "Sounds okay." He is beginning to regret breakfast.

Dan swallows two more Tootsies as fast as he can get the wrappers off of them. "Bet yer curious why a guy like me's driving around with a load of meat parts, heh, heh. You should see that damn stuff. Cow feet, pig heads, turkey guts, horse knees, shit like that. Make most folks puke, but not me." He drinks from the pint, and brown eddies swirl into the green liquor. "Don't bother me, no sir. Ya might say I'm an opportunist. I'll take a buck just about anywhere I find it, heh, heh, s'long's it's legal, more 'r less. Lemme tell ya, boy, gold's the ticket. Guy can make a fortune, if he's smart." The pint returns to Rupert. "That's why I took this haul. What I make off this goes straight into Maple Leafs. Heh heh, heh, buy low, sell high, that's what I say. That's the damn secret." He farts.

Rupert looks into the bottle, and shudders. He pretends to drink, then hands it back. Py has been pretending to sleep, only with one eye cracked open. At the sight of the vodka, he makes a retching sound. "Stop that, smartass," Rupert whispers. Py just grins.

Dan reaches for another Tootsie. "What was that? Hey, that damn lizard ain't sick, is it? If it is, hold it out the window; lizard pukes on my seat, I'll kill the damn thing."

"He's alright. Just coughs in his sleep. I think he might die pretty soon, anyway." Py gives the amphibian version of a Bronx cheer.

Dan laughs, and the echo sounds like a thousand voices. "Yeah, and it snores, too."

Dan drains the bottle, and expertly lobs it out the window, up and over the cab into the back of the dumper. "Never miss, heh, heh. Bet I got thirty empties back there, just since Denver. Funny thing—can't seem to remember a damn thing about Denver...."

Thirteen Tootsies later, the dump truck sails down the off-ramp to Ludlow at seventy miles per hour, its red hot diesel screaming for mercy. The airbrakes lock in with the sound of a monstrous, tormented cat and the truck fishtails. Dan rides like an obscene bronco buster, whooping and hollering and slobbering and thumping the dashboard with a hand the size of a pig's liver. The truck slides sideways across a cattle guard, past a stop sign, over a two lane road; it tips, tries to roll, rights itself, turns three complete 360 degree revolutions, bumps through a ditch, and comes to a dusty rest in the parking lot of the Beast Brothers' Grub and Grease 24 Hour Truckstop, Weigh Station and Wholesale Liquor Emporium. A dust cloud settles in behind them carrying a weird symphony, like a rousing applause from a long way off.

Rupert lies fetal on the floor, his new knapsack clutched between his knees. Py has crawled into his shirt and recites Hail Marys into a sweaty navel.

Dan laughs through a mouthful of chocolate. His belly convulses like a jelly waterbed in an earthquake. "Hot damn, made it again! Whatcha doin' down there, Bert? C'mon, this place's got the best damn lime-fudge pie in twelve states." He oozes out of the truck and toward the diner.

Rupert steps gingerly down, his face the color of bleached bone.

-25-

Felo-de-se

The cat sat, stone still, on a flat basalt slab in the center of a ruined temple. In spite of a full moon, it was invisible against the black rock. It watched the golden moon ascend the Zodiac, waiting. Silence dug in, as deep as a grave. A white horse stomped at the ruin's edge, uneasy. Winter constellations gleamed like silver rivets in black leather. A meteor streaked into blackness. The cat blinked.

The sun, cold and tired, came late. The cat was gone.

-26-

A Number of Beasts

The diner hums with the vibrations of noisy cowboys, smoking, sucking coffee and lying to each other. Stetsons, Tony Lamas, Levi's and tooled belts abound. An unreal atmosphere hangs like the curtain at a puppet show.

A lone, harried waitress avoids their leers and grasps, a loose cat in a kennel full of hounds. Her right arm strains against a heavy load of hamburgers, hotcakes and chili. A steaming pot leaps about with her left hand, splashing into random cups with amazing accuracy. A thin man with a huge hat pinches her butt. He yelps as his lap fills with hot coffee, and the faceless crowd around him howls with laughter. Ghostly laughter echoes back to them. The waitress deals her plates like a card shark, hustles back to the kitchen.

Rupert opens the neck of his shirt and warns Py to lay low. Just inside the door, he looks around for a fat, familiar face. An exceptional whoop rises above the din, and there's Dan, half standing in a booth across the room, waving his arms wildly above his head and gesturing for Rupert to join him. Rupert weaves through the crowd, one arm pressed tight to his lumpy stomach.

"Howdy, Bert, sit yerself down." Dan scratches his ear. "I already ordered for me; she ought'a be back pretty soon. Have whatever ya want; I'm buying. Get an order of flies for the lizard, heh, heh." Dan fills his entire side of the booth to capacity; Rupert slides into the other side.

A short old cowboy with a yellow mustache and an inch of smoldering Camel slaps Dan's meaty shoulder. "Danny boy, you old cocksucker! Ain't seen yer ugly hide in a coon's age! How's truckin'?" Steam rises from the crotch of his worn jeans. He plucks at the fabric with exaggerated care.

"Harry, you stupid bastard. Gimme a smoke. This here's Bert. Just looks like a damn hippie; really he's a good old boy, heh. Got the damnedest lizard you ever saw." Dan taps the cigarette against his thumbnail. "Give old Bert here a smoke, Harry. Wanna smoke, Bert?"

Harry slinks in next to Rupert. He pries a bent Camel from its abused pack. "Here, son. Think you can handle it?"

"Think so. Thanks Harry."

The waitress appears with a whole pie, brown and green swirls competing for space. She drops it in front of Dan and turns to the other two. "What'll you have? Chili's okay today."

"Just some java for me," says Harry.

Rupert reads her name, Philomela, from the tag riding high on the crest of her left breast. "Philomela," he says. "That means 'nightingale,' doesn't it?"

"Beats me, pal. What'll you have? Ain't got all day."

"Got knackwurst?"

"No, but there might be a couple of dogs back there, steamed in beer. One side Polish it is. Anything to drink?" Rupert shakes his head; Philomela vanishes.

Dan shovels pie to his face with rabid glee. His entire attention is focused on the eating.

Harry lights Rupert's cigarette with a turquoise encrusted disposable lighter. "Dan here's a hell of a nice guy, for an asshole, but he don't like nothing he can't eat. 'Cept gold, that is. Him an me go way back, used to partner a placer mine back in '80, '83. Then we had a rig together, I think, but I quit for some serious prospecting. Danny just keeps on truckin', and he swears he's gonna come up rich a'fore I do. Dumb bastard." He lights a third smoke from the butt of his second.

Philomela flashes by, drops a sausage and a squeeze bottle of mustard in front of Rupert, fills Harry's cup, then skids to an abrupt halt, eyes wide. "Hey, Red, what the hell's wrong with you? You got a big lump moving around your stomach!" She takes two steps back. "You're not gonna blow up like that guy in 'Alien,' are you?"

A blush creeps into Rupert's face; he looks sheepishly at his belly. "Uh, no. I'm fine, it's just... Can you keep a secret?"

A grin has frozen into a terrified grimace beneath Harry's mustache. His eyes are pasted to the squirming bulge. "'Scuse me, folks, gotta go." He comes unglued, races to the restroom.

Frightened but curious, the waitress moves a bit closer. "Okay, what secret? You better not blow up, now."

"Sure," says Rupert. "It's just my friend." He pulls open the bottom of his shirt and a grinning orange head emerges. "Philomela, I'd like you meet Py."

"Hey, you can't have no pets in here, we'll lose our license for sure."

"But he's not a pet. He's my friend and my teacher. We're really very close."

"Looks like a newt to me. Yuk."

"Now you've hurt his feelings."

"No harm done," says Py. "Pretty girls can call me whatever they wish. May I call you Gale?"

"Hey! It talks!" She sits down in Harry's place. "Hi there, little fella." She strokes the salamander's head. "You're cute. Sure, you call me Gale."

"Don't mind Rupert, honey. He can be a bit dense, but we get along all right. You wouldn't happen to have some sort of insects around here, would you? I'm famished."

"You kidding? This is a truck stop. C'mon, I'll show you where the flies are having their Mardi Gras."

Py slithers out and into Philomela's lap. "Can we bring Ru along? I promise he'll be good."

"Sure. C'mon, Ru. Bring your dog, you can eat with Py."

Rupert stubs out his unsmoked Camel, and watches the waitress's liquid stroll toward the kitchen. The diner's tumult seems buried below an expectant hush, a hush that seems to descend from a great height. She holds the salamander tight to her bosom and they chat like old friends. With sausage in hand he follows, more than a just a little jealous, more than a lot confused.

-27-

Wisdom, Again

Master:
Of course, games mean nothing when nothing is
at stake.

GIL:
You bet your sweet ass. Now play.

-28-
Some Odd Luck

"Sure, honey." Philomela leans with her elbow against a stack of empty green buckets. "I meet lots of horny young studs like you." She fiddles with the bodice of her uniform, snaps her chewing gum, half-smiles.

Rupert blushes, looks away. "No, I didn't mean it like that. I mean, well, what I meant to say is, well...."

Py pauses in mid snag. A fat fly struggles against his sticky tongue. "Right, Ru. What you meant was, Gale's got a tight nut, and you'd really like a chance to unscrew it." He winks at the waitress.

"Oh, jeez." Rupert turns and walks deeper into the alley, kicking at the odd bits of trash.

Philomela grins at the salamander. She fires a petulant tongue at Rupert's back, then lifts her skirt. She is wearing low-cut silk panties, black, with a red eye embroidered over her *mons venus*. A pyramid pupil glares mockingly at Rupert.

Rupert turns back, but the eye's gingham lid has shut.

The desert wind blows through the alley, sounds strangely like a chorus of "oooohs."

"Break's over," says Philomela. "Gotta get back to work." She picks Py up from his perch of rancid steak trimmings, cradles him like a baby. "Cute little Py. Sure you don't want to stay here with me? I got a duck pond at my house and with the diner here, you'd never go hungry." Her blue metallic eyes sneak through a mass of blond curls for a peek at Rupert. She leans her head close to Py and whispers. They break into controlled giggles. The salamander gives her a moist peck on the cheek, then hops from her arms to Rupert's shoulder.

"Well, Ru, what do you think? That's the best offer I've had since Colorado. Wow, like a duck pond, even. You wouldn't miss me a bit."

Rupert's aorta twists into a knot. "Come on, don't talk that way. I know how much you hate the road; if it's what you really want, then stay." He looks at the waitress and her smirk wounds him. Blood flows from the gash in his confidence. He looks at his feet. "She'll be good for you. Man, I'll miss you, well, I mean, after all, we're...."

Waitress and amphibian share a conspiratorial grin and a gusty laugh. "Don't embarrass yourself further, Ru. I'm not going to abandon you, not just yet. Somebody's got to watch you so you don't get bombed stiff and ruin Aleis's party."

Philomela giggles anew.

As they walk back through the kitchen, Rupert struggles to make the connection that he knows is there. Something about the way she rolls on oiled bearings when she moves. Something to do with the metallic sparkles in her winking eye. Something... something weird and surreal.

In the happy din of the diner the frustrating thoughts are flushed from his conscious mind; they swirl and gurgle down the drain into the septic tank of dreams.

Philomela transforms instantly into a coldly efficient waitress. It seems as if the time in the alley hadn't happened. Rupert's just another customer.

Py climbs into the neck of Rupert's shirt and snuggles in at the beltline.

Back at the table, Dan licks crumbs from an aluminum pie plate. Two others, mirror clean, nestle at his elbow. Harry slides deeper into the booth with a wary stare.

"Howdy, Bert. Dan told me about that sick orange lizard. Damned weird kind'a pet, you ask me. Siddown, we're about finished."

Dan sets the plate aside with a belch that turns into a sigh that turns into a deep, rumbling fart. "Howdy, Bert. Have a nice lunch? Best goddamned lime fudge in twelve states. Hey, well, got some bad news for you, son. I'm taking Harry here out to his new claim near Barstow;

you're gonna have to find another ride. Nothing personal now, it's just that Harry and me go way back. 'Sides, if he accidentally strikes it rich after I give him a ride, he'll have to cut me in, heh, heh." He wriggles out of the booth, like a bloated snake shedding its skin. "Tell you what, though, maybe we'll crash this biker party of yours, and between the three of us, we'll show them fairy suckers how to drink! Heh, heh, we'll drink the dumb bastards dry, right?"

"Sure," Rupert says, "just follow the pie plates with pyramids on them." From inside his shirt comes a muffled groan.

Dan pays the tab and heads for the door marked Beast Brother's Wholesale Liquors. "Time to stock up, heh, heh. Get you something, Bert?"

Rupert watches Philomela clearing a table with an almost magical grace. The uneasy feeling returns. "Uh, sure. A pint of whiskey, if you really don't mind. I'll get my gear out of your truck."

A few minutes later, Rupert sits on his new pack, playing "Your Cheatin' Heart" on his copper flute. Py naps around his neck, tail in mouth. Dan and Harry weave toward them, laughing and spitting. They are both heavily burdened: Dan carries a case of lime vodka, Harry, a stack of Tootsie Roll boxes with several cartons of Camels balanced on top.

"Well, Bert, been nice trucking with you. Shouldn't be too hard to hook a lift from here, lots of traffic, heh, heh." Dan sets his load on the running board and gives Rupert a friendly thump on the head. "Be sure to tell your girl friend about me, if you're not afraid of losing her, that is. Heh, heh. C'mon, Harry. See you at the party, Bert. And watch out for that lizard. One of these days it's liable to turn on you."

The dumper's big rear dualies throw dust and burnt rubber into the hot air. Portions of deceased farm animals jump about in the back like popping corn. A few pieces escape, generous handouts for the flies.

Py comes half awake. "Good riddance to the fat asshole. Why the hell did you have to invite those losers to Allie's party?"

Rupert drops his flute into the bag and starts for the freeway entrance. "Dan invited himself. What do you care, anyway?"

Dan's truck has been describing donuts in the parking lot. It straightens out and lunges for the onramp. Rupert scrambles to get out of its path, falls over backward into a weedy ditch. As the truck roars past, a small paper bag launches from the passenger window. A loud line of heh-heh-heh dopplers into the distance.

Rupert crawls out of a stunned semi-consciousness. Tiny hands slap his cheeks and an orange voice pleads, "Come on, Ru, buddy, snap out of it. You're okay, come on now, just sit up a little bit." The world begins to focus; Rupert rises to his elbows. "Here," says the orange voice, "drink some of this. Miracle it didn't break, that fat son of a pig. Here."

Rupert takes the pint in shaky fingers and coughs down a huge mouthful of whiskey. He sits straight to catch his breath. "Wow. What a trip."

"You all right? Anything broken?"

"No. I'm fine. I think." He pulls a thorn from his palm. A spot of blood wells up; he sucks the wound. He stands, wobbly, and brushes dust from the seat of his pants. "Let's try and get out of here."

The Mojave sun beats mercilessly against the blacktop. Heat waves shiver the air. Small rust colored clouds spot the distant horizon like puffs of eraser dust. Occasional ocher patches and misty clumps of sage are the only relief from the redness of the scene. Even in the closed eye, green after-images crouch impotent against a wall of scarlet. No life can prosper in this place; the only movement is a sporadic line of mechanical beasts, hermetically sealed and artificially cooled camels that speed blindly on, unwilling to stop for anything short of death, or gasoline.

Rupert's thumb begins to sunburn. His new clothes are dusty-red and soaked with sweat. One back pocket hangs torn and limp, and various barbed weeds cling to every square inch of cloth. Rodents could happily nest in his hair. Sweat rivulets leave muddy tracks down his face. Tired from complaining about the heat, Py has crawled into the depths of the knapsack and hides in the stuffy shadows.

To amuse himself, Rupert watches the Beast Brother's parking lot for a glimpse of Philomela. Finally, he sees what must be her, a doll figure among the giant sleeping trucks. She makes it to the edge of the lot and unlocks the door of a rusty, dented car, a rounded antique that leans drunkenly to port. Rupert hopes that she will come his way, that at least she will wave, but it is not to be. The old car rolls, unhurried and stately in the other direction towards a doubtlessly serene life, a duck pond. He thinks he sees one tiny hand extend from the window, waving. In this heat, he cannot be certain.

The same disturbing feeling boils to the surface of his brain. It has the quality of a remembered dream, a deja vu, but Rupert knows that can't be. He has never been to Ludlow before, has never even passed this way. He decides that it must be the combined effects of the whiskey and the heat, so he drains the last two fingers from the pint.

Across the freeway, a monstrous cloud of dust appears, exploding toward Rupert with alarming speed. He shields his eyes with his hand for a better look. The cloud stops abruptly at the freeway's shoulder. Red dust roils and billows away, unveiling dark and menacing shapes. Rupert's jaw unhinges.

Not more than a stone's throw away, four demonic war engines stand, rumbling and hissing like apocalyptic horses.

-29-

The Sick Lieutenant's War

The dust settles. A motley assortment of vehicles pulls into an arc behind the tanks.

"Hey, Py. Wake up." Rupert reaches into the pack and yanks the salamander out.

"Yow! What the fuck's going on?" Rupert says nothing, just raises Py up to face the task force. "Holy shit."

They stand frozen and silent, waiting for something unpleasant to happen. After an interminable moment, one tank creeps forward. It rolls onto the shoulder of the freeway, stops. The top hatch flips back and a uniformed man with a peacock feather in his cap climbs half out. He smokes a yellowed Meerschaum pipe. He inhales deeply and holds the smoke in.

A rush of smoke and a commanding voice snap Rupert to attention. "You. Hippie. Come here."

Rupert shoulders his pack, hefts his stick and takes a grim breath. Py takes position on top of the pack. "Guess it's too late to run for it," says Rupert. When a break in traffic comes, they set out across the road, with the resolution of condemned men. They stop a short distance from the muzzle end of the lead tank's howitzer.

"I say there," says the man with the feather. "Sorry if I've startled you, but I could use your help. Seems we've gone a bit off course. Have any idea where we are?"

Rupert releases a long held breath. "Uh, well yes, I think. Sort of."

"Splendid! Climb aboard. We can discuss it over a friendly peace pipe." The officer gives Rupert a gloved hand; up Rupert climbs. "Lieutenant W.B. Siques, commanding the Sixth Mobile Calvary, United Fucking States Marine Corps, at your service." He passes the pipe to Rupert.

"My name's Rupert." He sucks in a cloud of rank smoke.

"And I'm Py," says Py. He removes the Meerschaum from Rupert's shaking grip, takes a salamander-sized toke, and grins. "A pleasure to meet you, sir."

The Sick Lieutenant doffs his hat with a European flourish. "The pleasure is reciprocated, although I must admit surprise at my first polite amphibian. From your colorations, I would guess: a glorious specimen of Giant Pacific Salamander, Genus *Ambystomia*. Bit off your turf, I'd say."

"You flatter me, Lt. Siques."

"Not at all. Now, Rupert. This is actually quite embarrassing. A Marine detachment lost? If we radio for help, they'll laugh us into the Navy. Another toke?"

"Thanks. You're not really very lost, you know. This is the old Route 66 and that's Ludlow over there. Where you headed?"

"Nowhere special. Routine maneuvers, that old saw." He pinches a large chunk of oily black hashish from a brick in his shirt pocket, rolls it between his fingers, drops it into the pipe. He provides a light from a luger-shaped butane lighter. "And where, may I ask, are you going?"

Rupert's lungs threaten to explode under the impact of acrid smoke. He coughs and his eyes water.

Py answers. "We're going to a party at Big Bear Lake. Know where that is?"

"Not exactly. But I've heard.... Wait a minute, now here's an idea! If you'd like, you can ride with us. We'll take you right there. By God, that's a marvelous idea! Should be smashing fun! What do you say? Are we invited?"

"Well, we wouldn't want to impose, or get you in trouble, or anything...."

"Not to worry! We're already AWOL by now. As long as we're already in dutch, we might at least have some fun. Please?"

"Okay, if you insist," says Rupert.

"We'd love to have you," adds Py.

"Splendid! Watch your step, and welcome aboard." The Sick Lieutenant disappears down the hatch, and Rupert cautiously follows.

The inside of the tank is filled with smoke. Empty Harp's Lager cans teeter on every flat surface. A canvass gas-mask bag brims over with assorted pills and capsules on the gunner's seat.

"Rupert," the Lieutenant says, "I would like you to meet Batman. The zombie in the corner's name is Cooper. We've been playing a little game, and Cooper is losing. Oh, and Batman, the orange chappie's Py."

"Howdy," says Batman. He chain smokes low-tar cigarettes and his feet tap a complex rhythm.

The Sick Lieutenant has taken over the driver's seat. "Excuse me for one moment, please." He fiddles with the radio, and when the squeal dies down, speaks into the microphone. "Botticelli to all units, how do you read?"

From the speaker comes a clear voice. "Oh, c'mon, Lt. We're ten feet behind you for chrissakes."

"Ah, yes. Ahem. Very well. Course correction, stand by."

"Standing by, sir."

The Lieutenant puts his hand over the mike. "Nothing but a lot of smartasses. So Rupert, it's up to you. Which way to this Bad Bear Lake?"

"Uhm, let's see... south by southwest, about fifty miles. As the crow flies." Rupert looks at Py; the salamander nods.

"Botticelli to convoy. Course correction, mark: 44 degrees by 06 minutes. Fall in, you pussies!" He jams the tank into gear, and with a shrieking lurch it wheels and charges straight into the desert. The other vehicles execute a clumsy dance, and pull into a crooked line behind.

"Botticelli? This is Dog-breath. Where the hell we going, Lieutenant?"

"Butch Boy to Botticelli. Ditto. We're already AWOL."

"Lieutenant, Cruiser here. Headquarters is gonna be just a little bit pissed off at us, especially with the you-know-whats aboard. Over."

The Lieutenant fills his pipe with one long golden flower bud, fires it, and hands it to Rupert. He sighs. "Is this any way to treat orders from a commanding officer? Rupert, I long for the days of blind obedience, when jackass grunts would follow their officers to hell, without so much as a single whinny." He thumbs the mike on. "All right, enough already. Botticelli, here. Everybody listen up. We are taking a slight detour. We've been invited to a party at Bed Bug Lake. We're going to attend. If any of you fairies are scared of a few demerits, then you can just go home, wagging your tails behind you. See if I care. Over."

"Cruiser again. Sir, I don't mean to question your authority, but do you have any idea what they'll do to us if we disappear with the you-know-whats?"

The Sick Lieutenant presses the microphone against his stomach and twists around in his seat. "Batman, would you be so kind as to hand up a couple of beers?" To Rupert, he says, "It looks like I'm going to have to get tough. Sorry you have to be witness." He brings the mike back to his lips, and with a bored look screams, "CONVOY HALT!" He hauls back on both brake levers with all his strength, and the tank skids to dusty stop.

"NOW LISTEN YOU SORRY BUNCH OF HOMOS, I DON'T GIVE A FLYING FUCK ABOUT HEADQUARTERS! THIS TANK IS GOING TO A PARTY! I AM NOT EVEN A LITTLE CONCERNED ABOUT THE FUCKING-YOU-FUCKING-KNOW-FUCKING WHATS! ANYBODY WHO'S INTERESTED, FOLLOW ME! EVERYBODY ELSE, EAT SHIT AND DIE!!!" Then, as afterthought: "Botticelli, over and out." He rips the microphone from its socket, and flings it out the open hatch.

Rupert opens two Harps and hands one to the Lieutenant.

"That's telling 'em, Sickie," says Batman. He plays a little slapping drum solo on his thighs.

The Lieutenant giggles. "I guess so." He shoves the levers forward, and the tank lurches back into motion. "Anyone coming with?"

Rupert climbs up and takes a look out. "That rocket launcher thingie and one other tank. All the rest chickened out. Are you sure you're not going to get in a lot of trouble over this?"

"The point is, Rupert my friend, that I really don't care. Eventually, I suppose they'll have to come looking; we're carrying three fully functional nutes." He takes a long pull from his beer.

Py looks up, interested. "Newts? Why would they worry about newts?"

Batman re-lights the pipe. "Nutes. Short for neutron bomb. They equipped us with 'em to 'simulate reality.' Cooper here's the expert on that stuff; he claims they're thirty kilotons each.

Hey, Sickie, what say we drop one on L. A.?
Who'd complain?"

"Now Batman. No need to get carried
away. At least not quite yet." He giggles again.
"Now that Cooper's passed on, we need one
more daring soul. Rupert, do you play
Botticelli?"

"Well, I've played a little. Py's the one
who's good."

"Splendid! There's just one teeny-weenie
twist: for every 'no' answer you get, you have to
eat a pill at random from the happybag. Makes
the game more interesting when there's
something at stake. Poor Cooper never was very
good at this."

Py settles in on the gunner's seat, next to
the grab bag. "I've got a 'C,'" he says.

Batman:	Okay, Py's "it." Now remember, we've got to earn the right to ask our questions. I'll try first. Who said, "Wow, this planet's got the spins?"

Py: That's easy. Copernicus.

Batman: Damn. Oh well. I hope I get
            a Valium this time. One
            more hit of speed and I'll be
            ricocheting around here like
            a Teflon bullet.

Sick Lt: Hmm. Boys, Py's gonna be
            tough to beat. But I think
            I've got one. What's green
            and wears a beanie?

Py: I've no idea. You're in.

Sick Lt: Ha! Got you! It was Cecil
            the Seasick Sea serpent.
            Okay, we're in. May we
            assume that you're living,
            dead, or fictional?

Py: Yes.

Rupert: Living or dead?

Py: Yes.

Rupert: Oh-oh. This is where I
            always get into trouble. Are
            you living—no, change that,
            are you dead?

Py:	Maybe.
Batman:	What do you mean, maybe? Do you mean that you just don't know? Or do you mean that you know this man or woman or whatever to be both living and dead?
Py:	Yes to both. You're still in.
Rupert:	Are you Count Dracula?
Py:	No. But nice try. You're out.
Sick Lt:	O-boy! Rupert has to draw.

While Batman performs a dramatic drum roll on an empty can, Rupert extracts a largish pink capsule. He eyes it closely, and seeing it to be marked USMC, he shudders. He squares his jaw, sets his shoulders, closes his eyes, and pops it into his mouth. He swallows hard, with a generous shot of Harps and a resigned sigh close behind. The Sick Lieutenant claps, delighted.

Sick Lt:	Splendid display of courage in the face of overwhelming odds! Rupert, my lad, you're now an honorary fucking

	Marine, one of a few good men, from the Halls of Montezuma, to the shores of Bird Bugger Lake!
Batman:	We're still out. Okay, Py. What's made from a lamb, worn on ram, and knows every woman from here to Siam?
Sick Lt:	(Aside to Rupert) Batman's used this one before. Tries it on everybody once.
Py:	I give. I've got a feeling I'm not going to like it, though.
Batman:	And right you are! I'm Casanova's Condom!
Py:	Ugh.
Rupert:	Why do they call you Batman?
Batman:	'Cause I sleep hanging upside down from the rafters in the barracks. Makes my hair grow faster.

Sick Lt: We're in, aren't we? Let's
            see, all we know is that
            him/her/it is also
            living/dead/both. Are we
            either male or female?

Py: Both.

Rupert: Oh, come on. Who in the
            world could be living,
            dead, male and female, all at
            the same time?

Batman: Sounds uncomfortable.

Sick Lt: Think of the wardrobe
            you'd have to maintain.

Batman: But you'd only need one
            black suit.

Rupert: Boy, I think I'm already
            starting to feel that pill.
            Some kind of heavy pain
            killer, or tranq. Py! I know
            who it is! Aleister Crowley.

Sick Lt: Aha! The Great Beast! The
            Master Therion, Duke of
            Madness, Arch High Priest

	and Prophet at the Abbey of Do What Thou Wilt!
Batman:	Dirty pool. He was definitely male, and he's just as dead.
Sick Lt:	Don't jump to conclusions. Brother Crowley was quite resourceful. He claimed that he would beat death, and there were rumors that he was trying to come back as a woman. Wouldn't surprise me if he'd made it.
Py:	If only you knew.

Rupert climbs up the turret ladder and sits on the edge of the hatch. He tips his head back to drain the last drops of beer. Something catches his attention; he raises his hand against the desert sun's glare.

The tanks and the rocket launcher leave a trail of thick dust, a smoky wake stretching back for miles in a corkscrew plume. Hovering just above the plume, several hundred yards away, seven gnat-like dots flash on and off in the sun. Rupert watches them for a minute. They grow steadily larger.

"Your turn to be 'it,' Rupert," says Batman. "Think of somebody easy. That last pill has me hallucinating and I sure don't want to end up like that pussy Cooper."

The Mojave sun beats a slow-motion tattoo against Rupert's thickening brain. He feels his blood pressure drop. His stomach turns a queasy, labored somersault. A clear, gelatinous substance oozes from every pore, protecting his skin from sensation.

"Okay," he says, and the word comes back to his ears as a sluggish, low-pitch buzz. "Ehhhhg. Got an 'F.' Hnnng. Ugggn."

Py scampers up Rupert's pant leg and perches on his shoulder.

The radio begins to hiss and hum like an angry rattlesnake. "Dog Breath to Botticelli. Come in Botticelli. We've got company, Lieutenant. I think we're in big trouble. Come in Botticelli, please."

The Sick Lieutenant reaches for the mike from habit, and when he realizes it's no longer there, he turns backwards in his seat. "Rupert. See anything?"

"Unnggh," Rupert says. "Phhyssss ugnnsu, nnnnnnnnh."

Py answers for him. "Six, no, seven helicopters. They're coming up fast." He pulls on one of Rupert's eyelids, peers closely at the red network there, then tsk-tsks in disgust.

"What do they look like?" Batman squints up the turret. "Tadpoles? Carp? or Barracuda?"

"Five barracuda, two tadpoles."

Rupert switches to the opposite edge of the hatch, facing the oncoming threat. "Uhnnnn. Ah, mmmmm. Ugh."

Py translates. "I doubt they've come to escort us to the party."

Batman chews at the quick of one thumb nail. "This is bad, guys. If they look like barracuda, they're Apache gunships. Mean mothers." He searches frantically for the Meerschaum. "Two tadpoles means at least two officers. They must be serious." He finds the pipe and lights it with the coal of a cigarette.

The radio crackles. The Lieutenant adjusts the squelch. "Dog Breath to Botticelli. Come in, goddammit. What we gonna do, Sickie? Surrender, run, or fight? Talk to me Botticelli!"

The Sick Lieutenant stands half up from the controls. "Batman, you have the helm." As he moves to trade places, pressure is suddenly released from the throttle; the tank slows with a violent jerk.

Rupert flails backward. He grabs the nearest thing to him for support. The grips of a twin-bore, liquid-cooled .60 caliber automatic cannon reach for him like a helping hand.

The other rebel vehicles pull up alongside. A man with ear flaps, goggles and field glasses stands in the turret of the other tank. He yells through cupped hands. "Hey! Lieutenant! What the hell's going on? What we gonna do?"

The Sick Lieutenant wrestles with a large topological map. "Shit. We're still twenty miles from the mountain. We'll never make it. What do you think, Batman? Surrender?"

Batman drives hunched over, teeth clenched tight. "NUTS!"

A jackrabbit dashes in front of the tank; Batman swerves to miss it. "Wow! Did you see the size of that rabbit? Big as a fucking cow!" Beer cans, pills and other debris flash through the cockpit like a side-ways meteor storm.

Rupert swings wildly to the left. His fingers convulse around the trigger. Py grabs a double fistful of Rupert's hair. "Jesus!" somebody screams. The cannon fires, alternating barrels, in an exploding upward arc, 30 rounds per second. Rupert grips the bucking weapon as if it were a rebellious portion of his anatomy.

Sparks burst from the side of a flying barracuda. It tilts, then spins into a roiling cloud of dust, smoke and metal fragments across the desert floor. One tadpole flashes into a chrysanthemum of flame, and is no more. The man in the other tank's jaw plummets. He lifts his goggles, revealing a band of clean white flesh around his gaping eyes. A grin cracks his jaw shut. "WAHOOO!!" He cocks the action on his machine gun, then yells into the turret, "We got us a scrap!" He begins firing short, controlled bursts at the scattering helicopters.

Rupert's ammo has run out. He sits on the turret's edge, legs splayed, pop-eyed and breathing erratically. "Waaaaa. Unnnngh, hmmmmjnnnn, aaaaak." Py still hangs on with fistfuls of tangles red hair. When the cannon vibrations finally fade away, he cautiously opens one eye.

The Sick Lieutenant's head comes up between Rupert's legs like a perverse jack-in-the-box. "Hey, you guys, get down here!" He grabs one urine dampened leg and yanks. Rupert and Py tumble into the tank, Rupert's head bouncing off every step. They land atop the Lieutenant with a curse and a crash.

"Sickie," Batman calls. "What's going on? How we doing?"

The Lieutenant untangles himself. "By the Gods, we got 'em on the run! Rupert here's a bloody ace! Just keep driving; I've got to reload the 60." He drapes two ammo belts over his arm and heads up the ladder.

Py squirms out from under Rupert's groaning form. "What am I doing here?"

At the first sounds of battle, the U.S. Marine Corps Action Under Fire Hypnotic Training Program has begun to pay off. Cooper, with all the deliberate consciousness of a bludwurst, has crawled into an aft compartment. There, with only his feet protruding, he automatically goes about his duty to God and Constitution. By the time the Lieutenant has the cannon firing again, he has armed the trigger mechanisms of two neutron bombs, and is working like a robot on the third.

Py squeezes himself into Rupert's backpack, and pulls the drawstrings tight behind him. His last glimpse of the tank is dominated by Rupter's ash walking stick. No longer the bust of Anubis, it has taken the shape of a beautiful woman's face, the mouth open wide with burlesque laughter.

-30-

A Neutral Point of View

Ten miles away, where the Mojave Desert's flaming sand begins cooling into patches of green Lucerne Valley range land, Ruby stretches her abused back muscles. She massages both kidneys and stares vaguely into the desert air. She shakes a cramp out of her left thigh, squats beside the Norton to roll a smoke.

A distant rumbling wavers in and out of the heat. She stands and scans the horizon. A long ribbon of red dust curls into the sky from a point near the desert's edge. The point is headed straight for her.

"Goddamn stupid dune buggies."

She lights her crude cigarette with a wooden match and inhales a dense cloud. Glaring malevolently at the dust below, she flinches when two bright flashes of light appear at the column's head. Her smoke drops to the ground. A second later, muffled explosions rock the still air. "What the fuck?" With a small surge of adrenaline pushing at her heart, she fumbles through her saddle bags, drags out a pair of army surplus binoculars. "Jesus," she says. "Fucking tanks."

Through the field glasses, the scene becomes quite clear. Two tanks and another armored vehicle race along the bank of a deep dry wash. Behind them, two piles of rubble burn at the bottoms of pitch black pillars of smoke. Five shining helicopters hover high above both flanks. They drop back into an angry swarm, hold for a moment, then break into two groups and dart ahead of the armored column. Just out of range they stop, and turn to confront the armor. Six white contrails erupt from the choppers. Six pencil-straight lines become six fiery roses around the lead tank.

The war machines skid to a halt, in wedge formation. Both tanks fire their howitzers in low trajectory. A dense sheet of smoke boils up between the combatants. Tracer rounds begin stitching lines through the smoke into the helicopters. A flock of missiles leaps to the air like startled birds, dragging cones of smoke behind them. Another helicopter explodes; sparks of molten steel rain down to the desert floor.

The smoke screen expands, consuming ever greater chunks of real estate. Another volley bursts from the choppers, flashes of red and silver lightning rip through the bank of smoke.

Ruby realizes she has been holding her breath. Stale air and cigarette smoke burst from her lungs like a rocket attack. "Whooooooo-eeeeeee! Hot fucking damn!"

One of the tanks slides out of the smoke and sideslips into the wash. It skids, fishtails, then rights itself, careens full speed down the ravine ricocheting from side to side.

The helicopters seem to have missed the lone tank's escape. They continue the barrage. One last answering burst sketches dashed lines up from the smoke. A chopper's tail vanishes; it's body spins mad; it jerks to one side and slams into one of its comrades. Both dissolve into a fountain of ruin. A pause, then a sound like a gasp, then an arrhythmic applause.

The smoke curtain turns wispy, gray, unreal. Except for the smoke, there is no movement on the ground, no sign of life at all. The two surviving helicopters hover nervous, just beyond range. When the last murky ghost shreds away, they split up and drift closer from differing approaches.

The rocket launcher burns violently. Occasional explosions toss sparks into the sky. Three indistinct, man-like forms sprawl like broken puppets in the sand. The remaining tank has fared little better: turret shattered, one track loose and trailing, howitzer barrel twisted and limp. Miraculously, a man stands. His goggles hang about his neck. A pale band of flesh gives him a goofy, raccoonish look. He waves a white cloth about his head in the lazy eight symbol of infinity, surrender, and stock car racing.

The choppers swoop down to hover in front of him. They both open fire. One lonely leg twitches, as if trying to run.

The sound of the guns echoes like a chorus of boos. "Chicken shit!" Ruby bellows. *"Lousy muther fucker chicken shit!"*

Their noble work done, the helicopters flit about randomly, as if looking for something. Five miles from the scene of battle, the escaped tank climbs out from the wash, onto a paved two-lane road.

Ruby shoves the binoculars back into her saddlebags. She leaps astride the Norton, kicks it to life. "Get it man, go!" She wheels out onto the road and gives the bike its head. Her course, if she hurries, leads directly to intercept the tank, somewhat before reaching the town of Lucerne. She spits high into the wind, but is under it moving so fast that the gob falls a thousand feet behind. Her jaw clenches so hard her teeth bulge. Her eyes squint so hard they look like virgin anuses on the first day of a long prison term. The tendons on her neck form a flying buttress. Steam pulses from her nostrils; smoke from the Norton.

Ruby wants to help.

-31-

Resurrection

It is almost night. It is almost a full moon. It is almost a new millennium.

Twilight air sparkles and jitters above cool green meadow. Crickets chirrup, a nightingale whistles. The scent of recent rain hangs moist and heavy and sweet. A breeze purrs lazily by, barely ruffling the new realist stalks of tall grasses, the impressionist riot of wildflowers, the cubist silks of mad arachnids.

A black cat stretches and yawns on the upturned fender of an ancient automobile carcass. It tests its claws against rusting flakes. It licks its paws and straightens its face.

The cat jumps from the old DeSoto, rolls in the grass. For a time it plays tag with small white moths. The breeze picks up and seems to whisper something. Ears alertly scanning, the cat sits back in the grass, head a-tilt, whiskers twitching.

"Felony."

The air in front of the cat begins to shimmer; a golden light settles into the meadow. The light thickens slightly, becomes a solid translucent image. A young woman, a statue in purest gold, stands graceful and enticing in her own illumination. She's dressed in a costume from long ago, a peasant blouse and flowing skirts, long half-apron, sturdy shoes. Her sleeves hang loose and are rolled to just below her elbows. Her golden cheeks reflect the almost full moon. The statue hardens—opaque, solid, real.

The cat, purring like a well-tuned engine, rubs its face against the statue's ankles. Gold warms and softens, runs like happy tears down her cheeks. Drops of gold collect at the tips of her fingers.

On its side in a gully, the old DeSoto's rusty skin also warms and melts; it runs in trickles, leaving smooth bright metal in its place. Fresh rubber grows around newly born wheels, rich walnut forms along the dash, new leather emerges from rusty springs to grow into a perfect tuck-and-roll, midnight blue paint pools on the sky-side door and spreads like a caress to every surface, clear glass coalesces from the air into every frame; fifty years of entropy dissolves as the motor deliberately rejuvenates, cylinder for cylinder, nut for nut, wire for wire.

The girl, Felicity—now warm, robust, and lively—plays with Felony, the cat.

The old DeSoto, immaculate in rebirth, tips gently to its wheels and rolls out of the gully into the meadow, purring like a baby lion.

The almost full moon rides high in the night.

The old DeSoto's door pops open, as if by magic. Felony and Felicity climb in. There is a bouquet of wildflowers and a silver martini shaker on the seat. They roll across the grass like a golden ball on velvet.

It is almost a new millennium. It is almost time.

-32-
Chains

The Sick Lieutenant stuffs a long Cannabis bud into his Meerschaum with ritual care. He reaches for his lighter, but a leather-clad arm cracks like a whip and a wooden match flares over the pipe's mouth. He takes a toke, sighs and passes the pipe to the hand that lit it.

Fiery sunset bleeds through cracks in a derelict barn, paints tiger stripes on the tank's dusty bulk, and illuminates random portions of three figures lounging among drifts of hay. They pass the pipe in silence; lazy smoke drifts around bone gray rafters.

"Thanks again, Ruby," Batman says. "You saved our sorry asses."

"Aw shucks. Couldn't just stand there an' watch them fuckers blow the shit out'a you."

"No, seriously." The Sick Lieutenant blows a ring. "If you hadn't appeared when you did, the cavalry would've caught us long before now. That's certain." He straightens one leg and leans on his elbows. "Marvelous hidey hole you've got here, my dear. Simply splendid."

Ruby blushes. "Used t' keep hijacked trucks here. Those other guys gonna be okay?"

Batman looks over to where Cooper and Rupert lie, stretched and stiff. Cooper snores, but Rupert's glassy eyes stare into the great nothing. "Cooper's just zonked; he'll come around in a day or so. Don't know about that poor hippie, though. I think he's in shock."

Ruby stands, slaps hay from her leather butt and walks over to Rupert. "What's his name? He's fucking purty."

"That's Rupert," says the Lieutenant. "We picked him up hitchhiking. Delightful fellow. Knocked a pair of 'copters from the sky in one mighty burst. Had the most amazing companion, a Giant Pacific salamander named

Py. Haven't seen him since the engagement, poor little fellow. Missing in action, I suppose."

Kneeling at his side, Ruby places her lips around the Meerschaum bowl and blows a steady torrent of smoke out the stem and into Rupert's nose. He coughs, tears pour down both cheeks, he sits up as if propelled.

"Fucking-A. You live."

"Nnnnnnh, bletch schrug nugh'a." Rupert grinds his knuckles into his eyes. "Uhhhhhh."

"Don't make much sense." She sits close. "But damn, he's purty." She wraps her arms around his neck, snakes her tongue into the deep part of his ear. "Wanna fuck? Wanna run off to Tijuana an' get hitched?" A hooting echoes from the rafters, probably the wind.

"Aaaaaaaaaak." A shudder runs the length of him, whipcracks his feet.

Batman and the Sick Lieutenant giggle together for a moment or two. Batman pulls himself to a squat. "We gotta get serious, Sickie. It's almost dark; what we gonna do?"

"Well now, you're right, of course. We need a plan. Hmmm, let's see.... It looks to me like we've got but three options. One: we can ditch the tank and try for Mexico. Two: we neutron bomb L. A. and die heroes. Three: we continue with what we set out to do, and go to a party. Three's my personal favorite. I do so hate to let circumstance interfere with a good time."

"I don't know," Batman ponders. "I kind of like the L. A. thing. You know, surgery for a sick planet. 'Though I'm always up for a good time.... What the hell. Let's go to the party. We can always decide on heroics afterwards."

"Right-O! That's the spirit! Ruby? Would you care to join us? We're off to celebrate our victory over the powers of darkness. Love to have you along."

Ruby withdraws her tongue. "Sounds like a fuckin' gas. But only if I can bring Rupture, here."

"Why not? It's his party."

"Fucking-A. We'll follow on my bike. Keep you guys out'a trouble." She punches

Batman's shoulder —perhaps a bit too hard — grabs the top of Rupert's jeans and pulls him to his feet. "C'mon honey, we got a date."

Batman and the Lieutenant board the tank, carrying Cooper between them. Ruby slings Rupert onto the back of the Norton, then mounts. They leave the old barn, turning south into the Santa Anna wind. Ruby's taillight reflects against a round white object nailed to the door.

In the red light, the pie plate glows like a malevolent eye, a black pyramid its diabolic pupil.

-33-

The Next Limerick

There was a young fellow named Ru,

Who built wings of wax and then flew.

He was having some fun

When he flew near the sun,

And exclaimed, "What a dumb thing to do!"

-34-

Hyperfragments

Aleis stands naked at the center of a gray basalt slab. In a close circle around her, twelve black-hooded figures shuffle, heads bowed. Mammoth stones surround them in a larger circle still. Twenty-one bonfires crackle in a ring outside the stones. Beyond that, the black night, the cold stars.

She raises a bowl of fuming liquor to the full moon and calls in a clear voice, "Albertus Magnus! I summon thee! I call thee forth from thy foul abode in the center of darkness!"

From the sky answers a terrifying bellow. "WHAT THE HELL DO YOU WANT NOW?" A flash of green light and the very Earth trembles. "I thought I told you never to call me here!"

"Magnus." Aleis stands with legs in a solid triangle, fists on hips. "You lazy bastard.

Just one quick question and you can go back to the void. Where's the Stone?"

"I told you: Stonehenge." A fountain of putrescence erupts from the top of each monolith.

"That's where I am. Where's the damned Stone?"

The disembodied voice softens, raises in timbre. "Why should I tell you, anyway? You won't be able to handle it any better than I did."

"That's not your problem, Magnus. We've been over this before, goddamnit. I've already paid for it, now I want to know where it is."

"Paid me? Those were the scrawniest lambs I've ever seen. And in fifty years, I doubt I've used that DeSoto twice. Seems to have a mind of its own. Nice car, though."

"Look, you agreed to the terms. You should've bitched then."

"Okay, okay. But I'm warning you: that fucking Philosopher's Stone is a great big golden pain in the ass. Pretty much bankrupted me. Now listen close:

"When the full moon's right,

"And the shadow's light,

"In blackest night,

"And the arrow's flight,

"Painted white,

"Points to the might,

"Of the King's own...."

"Oh for chrissakes. Can the wizard act, Magnus." Aleis holds out both hands, palm up. "Just point, or something?"

"Philistine. It's buried there, six feet down." A bolt of purple lightning flashes from the clear night sky and explodes at the base of the altar. "And I hope you choke on it!" The twelve black robes jump back one step, in unison.

"Oh, and Aleis...." The voice has regained its thunder. "Just one little thing. My protection spell's about worn off. I'd watch where I sat down, if I were you." The voice dopplers into a maniacal laugh, leaving nothing but the stink of ozone.

Aleis steps down from the altar. "Here, Felony. Here, kitty." The black cat springs to her arms, purring.

In the shadow beyond the stone circle, a white horse tosses its head. It snorts a cloud of steam that dances with a will o' the wisp. It paws the mossy ground. The horse bares its teeth, and trots off into the blank of night.

Felony rubs her head against Aleis's chin. The witch claps her hands, thrice. "Everyone! Let's get busy. I want this pile of rubble in California by sunrise. And be careful with the Stone! Let's move!"

The chanting and the dancing and the incense and the howling and the screaming and the madness fill the moon's shadow until it rides bloated and bloody and dripping across the Zodiac like red melted wax, leaving trails and etched lines and incorporeal patterns in its tortured wake. Silent sheet lightning paints a grotesque shadow play among the monoliths. Subsonic moans rumble and vibrate. The Universe shifts three parsecs to the left. A sphere of air around the ruins warps into a thermoluminescent Klein bottle with a sickening kaleidoscopic motion. Light bends at awkward angles.

Stonehenge vanishes, leaving only a shallow crater and a clap of thunder to mark its passing.

-35-

Critical Mass

"It's about time," Aleis says. She touches the tip of her tongue to the last droplet in her crystal glass. "It all boils down to time.

"And of course, one hundred eighty-six thousand some-odd miles per second." She laughs a leprechaun laugh. A silver martini shaker appears in the air, shakes itself once and refills her glass. "The speed of light is immutable. You're standing on it."

The Sick Lieutenant stands at parade rest. The feather in his cap quivers, and Doppler-shifts from red to green. "Well now, I'm certain that sounds quite reasonable. But I rather doubt I'm following the logic. Please bear in mind that I'm absolutely ripped to the tits and would hardly be capable of following my own lead."

"Here comes a waiter. Grab a fresh drink; we'll sit somewhere and talk."

The waiter is stern and efficient. He holds his tray at just the proper height; the linen towel hangs from his forearm with just the proper plumb. The Lieutenant chooses a Scotch rocks twist and bows a precise six inches from the waist. The wooden waiter barely nods and clomps away.

Aleis indicates a direction with her glass. She takes a sip, links her arm in his and they move slowly through the thickening crowd. "Sickie, dear, what do you think of all this? How do you like my party so far?"

"Simply dazzling." He cranes his neck to see above the mass of people and other assorted beings, but can find no trace of any wall. "Though I must admit I'm still quite dumbfounded about this place."

She pats his hard shoulder. "Well, what did it look like from outside?"

"A large, empty circle of stones." He takes a long pull on his cocktail. "Damnedest thing."

"Right you are." She laughs again, and the sound of it is the sound of copper flutes. "And what does it look like on the inside?"

He looks straight up, and can find no ceiling. "Now that's what's got me worried. Either I'm closer to drug induced Nirvana than I thought, or I've died and gone to some baroque heaven. This room is bloody majestic! The only wall I've seen yet is the one I came through. And I seem to have lost that one."

"It is impressive, don't you think?" She waves to a small knot of Chinese Mandarins. "But don't worry, darling, it's a finite space. At least, I think it is. On the other hand, remember the entry way? I do believe that hall goes on forever. No good way to find out, of course. I sent out over a million invitations and everyone should arrive through different doors, but as to infinity... well, that's a difficult thing to prove." Aleis steers them toward a small group of revelers. "I want to show you to some of my friends."

Two men engage in a mild argument in the center of the group. The others watch with varying degrees of amusement.

"I tell you, Cthulhu was a goddamned wimp!" the taller of the two shouts through his pointy beard. He sees Aleis, and a sheepish grin possesses his face. "Allie, my pet, so sorry if I'm getting out of hand, but maybe you could settle this for us. Abdul insists on venerating those silly Elder Ones, even in this enlightened age. Don't you agree the modern demons deserve more respect than that?"

"That depends." Aleis hands the Lieutenant her glass, places her free palm flat against the tall man's heart. "Doctor, which enlightened age are you speaking of? In Abdul's Eighth Century, Cthulhu was quite worthy of his worship. You, on the other hand, are thinking in Sixteenth Century terms." She gently pats his cheek, and turns to the rest of the group, a twinkle in her eye. "Now, as this party exists completely outside space and time, neither of you has an axiom worth grinding. So just kiss and make up. I want you all to meet my new friend, Lieutenant W. B. Siques, USMC."

Pleasant greetings are murmured. Aleis pulls the Lieutenant into the center of the circle. "Sickie, this is Abdul Alhazred, author of the all-time inter-dimensional best-seller, *The Necronomicron*. To his left, Helen Blavatsky, Kate and Margaret Fox, Cornelius Agrippa — not to be confused with Jerry Cornelius; that's a different story altogether — and last but not least, the very eloquent Dr. Johannes Faustus."

"A privilege to meet you all, I'm certain."

Helen Blavatsky steps forward. "Allie, is this really your Sick Lieutenant? The hero of that terrifying tank battle?"

He bows deeply, doffs his hat, kisses Madame Blavatsky's hand. "At your service madam. You say you've heard of me?"

Abdul's mad eyes blaze. "Heard of you? We were pleased, no, I must say 'honored' to witness your moment of glory, the entire battle. You fought well enough to make Marduk Himself jealous. May you die well, my friend."

Kate Fox touches Aleis's elbow. "So where are ye hidin' that Rupert lad? Sure now, he must've come in with Sickie, here, eh?"

"Perhaps I should answer that," says the Sick Lieutenant. "Last I saw of him he was in the company of a rather splendid motorcycle enthusiast by the name of Ruby. My co-pilot Batman has elected to remain with the tank to await their arrival. I trust they'll be along shortly."

Aleis moves against him, squeezes his biceps. "Really now, darlings, I must mingle about and show off my Marine. Will you excuse us?"

As they wander back into the throng, Dr. Faustus is plainly heard: "Fuck you Abdul, Cthulhu was a pussy!"

They walk a relatively short distance. Aleis refills her glass, and the Lieutenant finds another. She extracts a long blue reefer, already lit, from a passing globe of Saint Elmo's fire. She puffs, then holds it to her Marine's lips. He sighs.

"So, is everyone here from a different century?"

"Of course not," she laughs, "but I tried to get a good mix."

"You've succeeded admirably. What was that about us being outside of space-time? Not that I doubt, from what I've seen."

"Here, let's sit." She waves her arm, and a dark red velvet settee materializes. They sit, she in the crook of his arm.

In the immediate vicinity, thousands of people stand, mill, sit, flirt, lie, drink, sleep, smoke, eat, belly-flop, sing, dance, joke, tease, laugh, swear, obfuscate, masturbate, intimidate, flutter, flatter, fluster, praise, play, and fall down. Yet the noise is somehow mute and subdued.

"Let me try and explain the physics," she says. "The stone circle outside is really just a sort of anchor. Actually, the party itself is a function of lightspeed. That places us in a protected zone, immune from those annoying disciplinarians, space and time."

"That's relatively simple." He sucks the joint down to a fragment. It vanishes in a pale blue flash.

"Okay then. There are at least two universes, probably more like ten, possibly infinite. The ones we know for sure exist together, like air and water. Only, between them there's an absolute barrier that normally prevents the inhabitants of one universe from crossing to the other."

The Sick Lieutenant coughs. "Like surface tension, right?"

"Exactly. That barrier is the speed of light. Since nothing that has mass can attain that speed, nothing material can break through. Only massless particles — energy — can do that. Do you follow?"

"Tentatively, yes."

"You're pretty sharp, Sickie. For a simulacrum." She winks. "Now here's where it gets weird. You know that all thought is based on electrical current, right? The charge itself is what we refer to as soul. If you separate the energy (soul) from the mass (body) the *energy* is able to pass through to the other universe." She plucks the olive from her martini and pops it into her mouth; the small sound echoes away into nothingness. "Now listen: when a living thing dies, its energy is released from the prison of its mass and attains instant lightspeed. And breaks on through to the other side! That's what everyone's really talking about when they talk about an afterlife. Subconsciously, humans have always known. Because it's the spark that actually knows things, and the spark is almost already there."

Colored light erupts from the air a small distance away. A punk rock band hangs over the crowd's heads, energetically murdering an old Doors' song. People up a mile away in every direction begin dancing epileptically.

The Sick Lieutenant flags down his waiter. "Wow. I'm still with you, I think, but how...." He picks out another glass of Scotch, and seeing a silver hypodermic on the tray, picks it up as well. "...I mean, how did you manage all this? And where on Earth are we?" He sniffs at the needle, deftly injects himself.

Aleis sips a fresh martini. "The how, my dear lovely man, is my own little secret, and, as I've already told you: we are nowhere on Earth."

"The other universe, then?"

A long happy laugh. "No, no, no. We dance along at the speed of light! This party is delicately balanced on top of the barrier!"

The Lieutenant, it seems, has found some potent heroin. He begins to nod, then jerks awake. "Splendid! Something occurs to me though. Didn't you used to be Aleist...."

"There, there sweet Marine." She stands and gently lowers him to his side. "You just rest a bit; I see someone I ought to talk with." She creates a pillow, slips it beneath his head.

She takes three dainty barefoot steps and travels three quarters of a relative mile back to an ornate arch leading to infinity. Standing just inside the arch, Dan and Harry carry on a conspiratorial conversation. Harry has a Camel burning in each hand. Dan clutches an empty pint bottle to his chest like it was a dying baby. His eyes bulge, and dart from side to side. Both men sweat, and shift their feet.

"You must be Dan, and you, Harry." Aleis says with a tiny grin. "My dear friend Rupert invited you, so you are both quite welcome. I'm Allie, your hostess. Do come in and be sociable. There's really nothing to be afraid of."

"Ain't a'fear'd o' nuttin'," says Harry. The cigarette in his left hand burns down to flesh. He jumps into the air, and yelps like a stepped on dog.

"Yeah," says Dan. "Just looking for my little buddy Bert. He here?"

"No, I don't believe he's arrived yet. But do come in. Can I get you anything to drink?" She snaps her fingers and the waiter instantly appears bearing a quart bottle filled with green viscous liquid, and a can of Burgie. "Really," Aleis says, "you two really must relax, or you'll never have any fun at all. I've heard so much about the both of you. Gold hobbyists, aren't you? Well we just so happen to have a gentleman who keenly shares your interest. Come along, I'll introduce you."

She takes one of their arms in each of hers, and leads them along the wall, chatting lightly. "This is really turning into a wonderful party, don't you think? I'm so glad you could come. Dinner will be served in about an hour, relatively speaking, and I promise it will be magnificent. You do plan to stay, don't you? Why, I've been working on this feast for over year—way over a year—and I think it's going to be just wonderful. Ah ha! And here we are!"

Aleis stops them before a gigantic hot tub. Sitting in the middle, surrounded by a giggle of underage girls, an old man with a long white beard inspects his fingernails. "Albertus," she says, "meet Dan and Harry. They're really quite shy, so you'll have to make them feel at home. Their favorite thing in the whole world is gold. And they'd just love to hear your gold story. Right boys?"

Albertus groans and sinks into the water up to his lower lip. His beard floats around his head like sperm attacking an ovum. "Oh my Gods." He rolls his eyes.

Aleis leans as close as she can and in a cheerfully dangerous voice whispers, "Listen, you old sod, party crashers deserve each other's company, and you better start being nice or I'll turn you into a pregnant warthog, so you can be uncomfortable <u>and</u> ugly." Then to the three together, "Please have fun, I'll see you all at dinner." As her smile leads her away, she hears old Magnus's tired voice say "So you want to talk gold, huh. I'll tell you all a-fucking-bout it."

She lights herself a cigarette with a tiny lightning bolt. She inhales, and inspects the hand-drawn rune on the filter.

"Hey, Allie! Hello!" The new voice comes from a small, gaunt man with scraggly beard and the sun blackened skin of a desert rat. He stands in the middle of a tight crowd, waving both arms madly.

Aleis changes course to meet him. "Hi, Josh. Long time no see."

"Too long, too, too long. Swell party; thanks for the invite. You know, I don't get out much anymore. Seems I intimidate people, for some reason. It's like, I'm a social leper, or something. You know? What am I, an authority figure now? I don't know anybody here, hardly." He separates from the crowd and gives her a warm hug.

She tilts her head down and kisses his forehead. "Why should you worry? You take your own fan club wherever you go." She indicates the group of men surrounding him. They've begun a chug-a-lug contest.

"What, these *schmucks*? You never in your whole life seen as many ass-kissers as I got following me around forever. Oy. John's the only one of the bunch I can even stand, and that's only because he's stoned out of his mind most of the time. So how've you been, anyway?"

"Fine, sweetie, just fine. Come on, let's go for a walk." She wraps her arm around his shoulder; he leans into her.

"So, Allie, how do you like your new life? Haven't had a chance to tell you, you look..." He pushes himself to arm's length, looks her top to bottom. "...divine. Uhm, I mean, not bad for a *schiksa*."

"Thanks, pal," she says. "I like it just fine. Might take a few decades to get used to the hormones, but I think I may have finally found my element." She flips her cigarette butt into the air; it dissolves with a sharp "POP."

"You know," Josh says, stroking his beard. "I like you better this way. You were such a cold *mensch*. And manipulative? In the old days, you would make a sheep of Svengali." He steps back a pace, holding both of her hands. "So tell me, one magician to another. How'd you pull it off?"

She laughs. "Really, I've done nothing as complex as what you did!" Aleis pinches the dark man's cheek. "No really, you'll always be the undisputed King. You want the Reader's Digest version? Or all the gory details?"

"Oh, tell me everything. I'm interested, you know. But I think I need some more wine."

The waiter appears as if from nowhere. Josh snags a silver goblet. "Thanks, Allie."

"Don't mention it. Let's see, now, where to start.... Okay. You remember that old alchemist asshole, Albertus Magnus? Well, he was way after your time, I don't know if you've heard of him or not. Anyway, back in the early 1200s he stumbled onto the Philosopher's Stone. By accident, must've been. He's too stupid to stumble across his own peter, if you get my drift. Well, the greedy pig went nuts, of course, and turned everything in sight to gold."

"Ha! Such a *putz*!"

"You got it brother. Anyway, one of the things he transmuted was this poor little hooker friend of his. He got to feeling guilty, I guess, and didn't melt her down, he just stashed her in a cave and sealed the entrance. I suppose he might've been thinking of her as a retirement account...." They laugh in the kind of harmony reserved for comfortable friends. "So I was looking for the Stone one day and found her instead."

"Ah, I get it. Perfect preservation makes great raw material."

"I'll say. The rest wasn't very hard, but it was fairly complex. I had to figure out a way to get to her while she was flesh, but if I just sent her back in time she'd've still been carrying her natural personality. And I really didn't want to kill anybody. Or I'd have simply stolen a live one in the first place."

They pass directly beneath the punk band. They're playing an ominous song about vampires.

"Wow," says Josh, "pretty sticky problem. How'd you get around it? Did you try animating her while she was still a statue?"

"No, not exactly. I thought about that, though. Would've left her with a new personality and me with the same problem. What I did was this: I sent her forward in time. You see? I sent her a ways past the point where the old me died. Then I set her personal chronosphere running backwards."

"No shit." He plucks at his beard. "You'd need a counter weight, I think. To keep her from shooting clean through the future, like gold through the proverbial goose, and out the far end. Right?"

"Right-O. You'll like what I ended up using. Turns out that a solid gold bar wench masses exactly the same as '49 DeSoto. So I sent them both off to the year 2000; the girl instantly, the car the slow way, naturally." She gestures wildly as she speaks; her crimson tipped fingers seem to speak a strange mystic language of their own. "Pretty cute, hmmm?"

"What do I know from cute? Einstein of the occult here; 'cute,' she says." The small, dark man points to Aleis's left, where the crowd condenses about some nucleus of interest. "What do you suppose that's about?"

"More entertainment, I'd bet." She smiles a sly smile. "Shall we investigate?"

"Please, let's do! That tank battle was a blast. Do you see the waiter anywhere?"

Aleis breathes out a tiny cumulonimbus. "Oh, allow me." The cloud drifts down to hover above his chalice. A puny clap of thunder, a brief downpour, and the goblet fills with clear water.

Josh waves his hand above the rim, then takes an exaggeratedly cautious sip. "Not bad. Chateau Blanc, 1357. Of course, I was shooting for Mogan David." They laugh again, and the sound of it is like the scent of an impending summer storm. "So what became of the DeSoto?"

She stops, turns to face him. "Strangest thing!" One eyebrow wrinkles. "The car and the golden girl met at midnight, 1999, just like they were supposed to: the girl as good as new, the car a pile of rusty junk. But when I quickened the statue, the DeSoto apparently rejuvenated itself! I can't figure it out. That car should've crumbled to dust."

"Hmmmm. Did you see this yourself?"

"No, I sent my familiar. But I trust Felony's powers of observation. She told me that they seemed somehow linked, the girl and the car."

Josh scratches his head. "Maybe the car's picked up a demon. You never know where those pesky Elder Ones are gonna show up these days. Or, well, you know major time tampering causes anomalies."

"It's not possessed. I've been driving it, now and then, and there's no sign of foreign personalities. I'm certain I'd know."

"Say," he says, "you weren't using real space, were you?"

"No, of course not. I set up an astral page. One half is superimposed over the Pacific Northwest, 1999. That's where I held my reincarnation. The other half is slightly out of the time stream, over the Mojave Desert. That one I'm using for the entertainment. Wouldn't do to hold a tank battle in real space, now, would it." A silver martini shaker floats alongside her right shoulder, patiently waiting for her glass hand to still.

"Ha! I've got it, then. You've been driving the DeSoto around the entertainment page, haven't you. That created a mirror image of the car in out-time. See?"

"Ho Josh! You're beautiful. Why didn't I see that? I build a mobius circuit, and don't even notice." She sips.

They reach the fringes of the thickened crowd. Two people separate from the mass. One, a tall handsome man in black tails twirls an ebony baton in greeting. "*Bon soir*! Allie, Joshua. Been looking for you!"

Aleis's eyes roll up into her head. "Oh Gods," she sighs. "Master Therion. Who the hell invited you?"

"Why we did. Don't you remember?" He laughs softly. "Come now. How could you expect me to miss this party? And besides, this presents the opportunity of several lifetimes!" He bows and takes her hand, lightly kisses the knuckles. "Lady Aleis, would give ourself the pleasure of a dance?"

"Love to," she says through clenched teeth.

The Master smiles broadly, then grasps Josh's hand and pumps it. "You'll excuse us, old friend, I hope. Why don't you and Glinda here just relax and watch the show; the next act is just begun. You can introduce yourselves. More chances to lie, that way." He pulls a silk kerchief from the air and drapes it over his right hand. He politely but surely draws Aleis into his arms.

She stiffens for a moment. Pale pink fog rises around their feet. It swirls between their legs and an Austrian waltz swirls with it. She relaxes, laughs two perfect notes, follows his lead on naked, nimble feet. They dance like newlyweds at the reception, like lovebirds eager to mate, like duelists from long acquaintance comfortable at either end of sharp swords.

Silent for an eternal second, she allows the music to float her along. She sighs and touches her forehead to the Master's cheek. "I should've known you'd turn up."

"But my dear, you did know. Practically by definition!"

"Then why don't I remember this meeting? No, don't tell me. I'm not about to start an argument with myself. I mean, with you."

"The point is, my lovely, that you wanted me to come. Why else would you have chosen to place this party in the only locale in all the Universes where our meeting is possible?"

"What would Freud think of this?" She lays her head against his neck.

"Curious thought. Well, literally we're just a transsexual with a temporally split personality, dancing with ourself. That's got to be a whole new form of masturbation, wouldn't you think?"

She nips the skin on the edge of his jaw, quite hard. "Crude bastard."

"We always were. Why did you drop 'Therion?'"

"What kind of name is that for a girl?"

"A poor one, I suppose. Want to go somewhere and screw?"

"I beg your pardon." She actually blushes, a gentle pink champagne colored stain that takes the form of a perfect death's head moth, then just as quickly vanishes.

"Oh come now. Don't pretend you're not at least intrigued. Wouldn't you like to know what it really means to fuck oneself?"

"Now *that* would be an entirely new form of masturbation." The waltz ends. Aleis disentangles herself and steps back. The pink fog dissipates. "I can't spend the whole evening playing with myself. Ourself. I've got to play hostess. Stick around for the banquet, if you must. I've got a few surprises lined up. But please, keep out of my sight. You make me nervous."

The Master kisses her hand. "As you like it, my dear, myself." He disperses like the fog, leaving only his smile. "Please make my apologies to Glinda." The disembodied grin shatters to a fine crystalline powder; a trickle of slow motion glitter sparkles to the floor.

Aleis makes the Sign of the Evil Eye and blows a Bronx cheer through it. She flinches at an eruption of laughter from the forgotten crowd, turns, threads her way into the thick of it.

The crowd watches a three-dimensional, twice life-sized image of an embracing couple. The woman is clad in dusty black leather and polished chain. The young man has both hands propped against her swelling chest; as he strains to lock elbows, his face contorts in a gargoylian rictus.

"Come on," says Ruby. "You know you want me."

Rupert's elbows lock, the strain proves too much for the zipper down Ruby's front. It bursts, and two perfectly magnificent breasts heave into view. Each is the size of Rupert's head, and punctuated by a delicate chrysanthemum of fiery crimson. Ruby and the crowd gasp in unison. Rupert stares, and for a moment, his struggles cease.

Aleis spots Josh and Glinda. She joins them. "How do you like the show?"

"Allie," says Josh, "you've outdone yourself. Where did you get the idea for that biker? That outfit, that attitude—and who'd have ever guessed at those remarkable tits?"

"I'd like to claim credit, but I can't. She's not one of the constructs. You know how an astral page tends to touch the real world at the edges? That's the only explanation I can come up with. Ruby just showed up."

Glinda claps her hands. "You mean she's real? How marvelous!"

Ruby has taken advantage of the lull in Rupert's defenses to cement her hold. She grips his head in both hands, mashing her breasts flat against him, smashing kisses into his face. "C'mon Rupture. Relax and enjoy it!"

Someone shouts, "Go for it, Rupture!" The crowd guffaws.

"Poor Rupert." Aleis shakes her head. "I really ought to go rescue him. I never meant for him to get involved."

Josh turns his eyes to look at her, without moving his head. "You mean he just wandered in, too?"

"Oh, rescue him!" Glinda bounces on the balls of her feet. "I so want to meet him, and we can't let him miss the party! Not after all he's been through." She twinkles with excitement. "He's been such good sport."

"Right enough," Josh says. "We'll all go. I'd like to get a close up view of this astral page of yours, anyway."

Ruby shifts her strategy, grabs a tight double fistful of Rupert's butt. She grinds her pelvis into his. "Dammit, Rupture. I thought all men was supposed to want it." She jams one hand into the front of his jeans. The tip of her tongue peeks out from the corner of her crocodilian grin. Rupert's eyes roll in opposite directions. He inhales six sharp gasps without exhaling. "Now yer getting it," she coos, and sticks her tongue into his mouth. Her hand makes rapid trapped-animal movements in his pants.

Aleis and Glinda each take one of Josh's arms. They strike out in a random direction, pushed on by a wave of laughter from the crowd. They wander through muted sounds of revelry, chatting about happy nothings, and other magicks. After 999 steps, they arrive at the wall; 666 more and they reach a massive vaulted arch. Wisps of yellow smoke drift through the open entrance, eddy into dark clumps, coalesce into individual giggling people.

Aleis nods, smiles, and welcomes the newcomers as they pass. She motions her two friends through the arch, finding it to be a portico on the other side.

"Is this the only way into the ballroom?" Josh's expression crinkles. "It looks just like where I came in, but I'd swear it was way back there, nearer the band."

"No." Aleis winks at Glinda. "This is the only door."

Josh searches nervously for landmarks.

"But this one door does occupy a surprising number of locations." Aleis laughs and Glinda titters. Glinda extracts a periwinkle cigarette from her elaborate coif. She takes a light from a small fire in the palm of Josh's hand.

A corridor runs parallel to the ballroom. Directly opposite the archway, two identical black walnut doors—banded in bronze and solid as Midas's vault—stand side-by-side. Twenty feet from either door, a row of single doors closed by parti-colored portieres begins. They are ten feet apart and continue with the corridor well beyond the limits of human vision.

"Jeez," Glinda sighs into a cloud, "and I thought I was a good witch. This sort of magick just boggles my brain. If there's only one entrance, but any number of exits, how does one know where one will appear?"

Josh frowns.

Glinda giggles. "Come to think of it, what could it possibly matter? The fun is everywhere!"

"Okay," Josh says, "out here, the hall looks like it runs straight as an arrow, forever. Inside, the ballroom seems round, if it has any shape at all. What gives?"

"It only looks straight. If you could see far enough, honey, you'd be looking at the back of your own head." Aleis strikes a contrived pedantic pose. Her voice changes into a man's thick accent, and a fluffy white mustache perches on her upper lip. "Zis hall," she booms, "ist un vour dimensional mobius schell, zat completely encloses der party, protecting zese premises vrom der radical absence of cause und effect zat occurs only at der speed of light. Mittout der hallway it vould be impossible to maintain any zort of form at all; even mit der hallway zere iz a definite tendency to chaos. I am zure you have all noticed: many things are pozzible at der speed of light." She claps her hands, spins lightly on one foot. The mustache and the accent are gone. "You pays your money, you takes your chances." She hugs Josh and Glinda together. She kisses Glinda on the mouth, then Josh. "My favorite old friend, and my favorite new friend. Isn't this fun?"

Josh slaps her behind. "Allie, dear, this is beyond a doubt the best party I've ever been to. Compared to the last Anniversary of the Pyramids? That one wasn't even in the same league. Atlantis, Schmatlantis. It took two centuries to get the smell of fish poop out of my sandals."

Glinda giggles like a tickled elf. "Oh, come now! It wasn't that bad. I sort of enjoyed the Procession of Eels.... Such pageantry! Anyway, shall we go find Rupert? He'll miss everything!"

Arm in arm they push through the left hand walnut door. They stand one step outside the monoliths of Stonehenge, formerly of England. A setting sun paints cubist patterns in orange and gold on the stones. Lodgepole pines whisper with birds and insects. A promise of rain perfumes the air.

Glinda draws a succulent breath, holds it until she quivers from the ecstasy of it. "Oh wow, this is pretty. Where are we?"

"Big Bear Lake, see? There's the Lieutenant's tank and over there, that foul dump truck." Aleis wrinkles her nose. "I think Dan and Harry were a mistake. They're not all that amusing, after all. Just gross." She leads them toward the tank's brooding mass.

Glinda makes a val-gal finger-in-the-throat motion. "Way over the top, darling, but I thought the diner scene was pretty funny."

Josh chuckles. "I'll agree that Dan is a bit too—should I say it—pulpy, but, oy, how he dived into those pies!"

Aleis sticks her tongue out. "I'm still sorry I made him."

As they approach the rear of the tank, an oddly misplaced voice hails them from the front. "Halt! Who goes there?"

Batman hangs by his feet from the end of the howitzer barrel. He holds a small machine gun at the ready and looks quite serious. His hair, longer now, brushes the dirt beneath his head.

Aleis holds her hands up, palms forward. "We come in peace." She blows him a kiss and winks.

"Allie!" Batman kicks his feet free and tumbles to the ground. He jumps up, takes Aleis's hand, clasps it tight to his chest. "It is a great honor to meet you at last, Master. Your wish is my commandment." His hair stands straight from his head, giving him a look of cartoonish surprise.

Aleis blushes. "Now, now. Let's have none of that nonsense. I'm really not that kind of master anymore. Just pretend we're equals."

Josh and Glinda introduce themselves, grinning. "You're kind of cute," giggles Glinda. "How come you're not at the party?"

"The Lieutenant went on ahead, ma'am. I'm just hanging around waiting for some friends."

Glinda wraps her arms around Batman's waist. "What a coincidence." She rubs against him like a cat. "We're looking for someone, too! Know where we might find a guy named Rupert?"

"Hey, that's who I'm waiting for. Last I seen, Rupert was with a woman named Ruby on a cool old Norton. They should've been here by now." Batman gulps, and tries to hide a conspicuous erection behind Glinda's leg. She rubs her thigh against it, giggles, and nibbles at his ear lobe.

Aleis hops up to sit on the tank's track platform. She crosses her legs and adjusts her skirt. She rolls her eyes, and begins buffing her nails with exaggerated aplomb.

Josh grins. "Ahem. So tell me, Batman, how's your friend Cooper doing?"

"Uh, um, Cooper... Cooper's in the tank. Been pretty much comatose for a while now. He'll be all right, I guess." Batman bites his own lip, and disentangles himself from Glinda. He looks guiltily at Aleis. "Uh, Rupert's probably back that-a-way a piece. I saw 'em turn off, no more'n a mile down that road." He swings himself up onto the tank, climbs into the turret. His voice come out the hatch all hollow and eerie. "He left his pack and this stick. Wanna take them?"

"Sure," says Aleis. She reaches out and grabs the walking stick by its head, the carved likeness of a salamander, rampant. She holds it toward Batman; he slides the straps of the knapsack over the end. The pack rides down the stick and over Aleis's arm. "Thanks, Batman. Why don't you go on inside? Have a drink, look around. You might be able to find Sickie."

Glinda *grande jettees* onto the tank. "Allie, you and Josh can look for Rupert; I think I'll stay and keep Batman company for a while." She twitters like the sound of porcelain ballerinas on a carousel. "I'll meet Rupert at the banquet."

Aleis shoulders the pack and hops to the ground. "Very well, sweetie, see you later." She takes Josh by the hand and as they strike off down the road she twirls the walking stick in a very amateurish way.

As they walk, Josh fingers his scraggly beard. "There's something I don't understand, Allie. You said that Stonehenge is your anchor, right? Well, if the party's traveling at the speed of light, what's the anchor for?"

"Maybe 'anchor' was a poor choice of analogy. Hmmmm. Well, damnit, it is an anchor, of sorts. Imagine a long string with a weight attached to one end. Spin the weight at the speed of light and anchor the other end of the string. That's what keeps us in some contact with reality, keeps us from shooting off to another universe or something."

"And that interminable hallway is the string. How many manifestations of Stonehenge are there?"

"As far as I can tell, they're infinite. Every door in that hall leads to its own Stonehenge and every guest entered through a different door. I imagine some of the more remote doors lead to some very strange places."

Josh stops suddenly and cocks his head. "Shhhhh. Did you hear something?"

Aleis shakes her head.

"I could swear someone just said, 'bloody hell.'"

"FOR THE LOVE OF POND SCUM, LET ME OUT'A HERE!!"

Aleis's eyebrows arch. "I heard *that*."

"Allie, I think it came from Rupert's pack."

A grin broadens her face. "Oh!" She gently lays the bag at her feet and loosens the drawstrings. A small orange head breaks into the opening, blinking and gasping.

"Jesus! About Bloody Time! Where the hell am I?" Py tosses his head about, both eyes drawing wild orbits of their own design.

Josh rolls in the dust, laughing and gasping for air.

"What's with you? I say something funny?"

Aleis pulls the salamander from the bag and presses him to her bosom. "Oh, Py! I'm so glad to see you. We thought you'd bailed out during the battle. Are you all right?"

The salamander's eyes focus front; the fight goes out of him. "Why, it's Aleis! I've been, uhm, hibernating. Ever since, ever since...." His eyes pop wide. "The battle! Jesus, what happened? Where's Rupert?"

"Whoa, calm down. Rupert's okay. We're trying to find him right now." She strokes the soft, peach-colored flesh beneath his chin.

"Batman and the Lieutenant are all right, too. It's hard to say about Cooper. Did you have a nice nap?"

Py yawns and stretches. He points his tail at Josh. "So who's the laughing hyena?"

"Joshua," she says crossly. "Get a hold of yourself. Haven't you met Py? He's my favorite amphibian in all the known universes."

Josh picks himself up and dusts himself off, still fighting for air. "Sorry, I'm sorry. Please forgive me, me, not laughing at you, really. But you said the funniest thing!"

"You'll have to excuse him, homemade wine goes straight to his head."

Josh quiets to irregular heavy breathing. "Whew! Sorry, again, really I am. It's a pleasure to meet you. I've followed your exploits with keen interest." He bows and extends his hands, palms up.

Keeping one eye on Josh, Py turns the other on Aleis, unblinking in either. "Yeah, okay Josh. Likewise, I'm sure." He turns his head to aim both eyes at a point between her dark eyes.

"Allie, how could you? You've been using Ru and me for parlor games. Haven't you." He turns away, makes a small spitting noise.

Josh looks quite startled; Aleis looks at her feet.

Py climbs to her shoulder, using fists full of hair to steady himself. "It's one thing to exhibit constructs like Dan and the Marines, but Ru? Goddamnit, Allie, when you first got me into this, you promised that all you were after was a simple reincarnation and the general advancement of magickal science. And now I find out you're selling tickets to a newt-sucking sideshow."

Still watching her feet, she pleads, "No, please don't think of it like that! Really it wasn't, I swear!"

"What the fuck should I think? As long as I've known you, I've believed in you and your motto: Do What Thou Wilt Shall Be the Whole of the Law. I just didn't dig that you think it applies only to yourself."

"Hey," Josh squeaks, "what is all this?"

"All what? I thought you were watching the show. Don't tell me you came in late."

Aleis sucks in her lower lip; tiny tears join to form a pond in each eye. She carefully sits cross-legged in the middle of the road. "Py, please. Josh didn't do anything. This is my fault; let me try to explain."

"Sure. Josh, sit down and listen to this. You might find it interesting. Maybe even *entertaining*." The salamander flops to the ground. He snaps up an unwary beetle, then settles into an elongated figure eight. "Let me tell you a little story, old man. It's about a frog prince. A real fairytale.

"Once upon a time, there was a great magician. His magick was powerful and he knew many things. He knew how to escape space-time by manipulating the speed of light. He knew how to tap sub-atomic energies to work impossible events. He knew how to conjure demons and spirits and knew all the Elder Ones by name. He knew everything there was to know about life and magick. He knew that every living thing must finally shed its body of matter and move on. He knew Death intimately.

"He knew about death, and he knew that in all the history of all the universes, no living entity had ever escaped. Sure, spirits live forever on the other side, and sometimes they can even come back over here for a short spell. But form, to a spirit, is only memory. Everything of flesh must die. The magician knew this all too well.

"Still, he was a mighty sucker. He thought that if he couldn't find a way to cheat the inevitable, who ever would? He resolved to try." Py pauses, slaps his tail into the dust.

"The Master Therion (for that's what our magician chose to call himself) began his experiments and eventually developed a plan. The Phoenix Affair was begun. He would create a simulacrum, breath it to life, then invade it with his own astral body, his soul, his mind. The simulacrum presented no problems for the Master, just a life-sized golem molded from dust. But there was a problem! It seemed that not even the mighty Therion—though he tried everything he could think of, again and again—could animate a cold lump of clay. First he was frustrated, then furious, and presently, he became desperately obsessed. He decided to enlist the aid of a higher power.

"The Master, in an amazing fit of hubris, summoned an Elder God. GIL, the giver of life Himself. Now GIL, it must be said, was not entirely happy at being called from the Divine Plane. But he was somewhat impressed with the Master's preparations, and academically interested in the processes at work. And so it amused the God to help. He sent a sprite that He imbued with the power of a single incarnation, and committed it to the success of Therion's golem in every way.

"For reasons of irony, the sprite was given the form of the fire-born. A salamander."

Josh looks at Aleis. She will not meet his eyes.

"So," says Py. "You begin to see light. Well, this is what happened. The sprite gave

Therion's simulacrum a spirit-goose: animated it. It was a good job, actually. The thing stood up, shook its head, looked right at me. I knew then that something unexpected had occurred. It seems that GIL had wrought a minor revenge: when I used the power and brought Rupert to life, I also imbued him with a soul of his own. Regrettable." He spits a fragment of beetle carapace.

"Well, that was just too bad for the Master. I wasn't going to let him push a healthy soul from its rightful body. And to be fair, I doubt he actually would have."

Aleis finally looks up.

"At any rate," Py continues, "the Master Therion didn't give up, he just set out on a different tack. I, on the other hand, had been committed by GIL to the success of the golem. Rupert. And really, I would have felt responsible for the lad at any rate. I animated him, by the gods, I would care for him, protect him, educate him.

"Poor Rupert. He never had a proper childhood. He was born full grown with an amphibian for a mother. I taught him as best as I could, but hell, I'm just a lousy sprite. What should I know about raising humans?"

Aleis starts to interject, thinks better of it, begins quietly crying in earnest.

"Meanwhile, Therion had gotten himself a new plan. He determined that time was the key. Living things cannot, of course, change their course through time. Inanimate objects, however, can be fired off willy-nilly, forward or backward through the timestream, as long the mass equation remains balanced. It remained only to locate a perfectly preserved body, perfect in every detail yet still inanimate—which he managed after a time—and then an appropriate counterweight. Next began a complex series of events designed to deliver a young, viable body ready for a new owner, with no pesky soul of its own to tweak the Master's conscience."

"Yes," Josh says, "I know about that."

"Then you are doubtless aware of the astral pages. Therion set the pages up for two reasons. One, to provide a secure environment for his project. Two, as a stage for the entertainment of guests invited to the grandest imaginable unveiling of his success, the Anniversary of the Pyramids party. He—or maybe it was 'she' by then—built a group of puppets strictly for the show. You may have met some of them, the Marines, that disgusting fat meat merchant. They have no will, no souls; they exist to entertain.

"Rupert and I were living on the Oregon page while I tried to teach him to be a people. After about a year, I decided it was about time to expose the lad to the real world. We left the Oregon page and spent a delightful year bumming about the American West. I kept trying to get him settled somewhere he could live like a regular guy, but he wanted to keep going, see everything. We went here, and there, and then I took him to Vegas, then we headed for California.

"I hadn't seen the Master in all that time, and apparently it was around then that the Phoenix Affair concluded. I had no idea of its success. I was also unaware of the location of the entertainment page.

"We stumbled onto the page, quite by accident, when.... Wait a minute. We didn't stumble anywhere. We got a ride from a lovely lady in an old DeSoto. Who drove us on to the page." He jumps into Aleis's lap, tiny fists clenched. "Damn you, Allie. You never gave a shit about Rupert; he's just a mistake to you, better minimized and forgotten. Whatever made you want to confuse and humiliate him? If I'd known it was you at the time, I never would've let him get in the car."

Aleis's eyes have dried, but there's no spark there, no sign of anything but gloom. "Py, please listen. You don't understand! You're right about the Master Therion. He never cared about much of anything save magick, and his own immortality. But the Therion is dead! He exists no longer in this time. Sure, it's his astral self and his mind inside me, but there's something else none of us expected. I'm a woman now. When I entered this body, I entered into a morass of strange hormones and alien emotions. I'm changed, Py, totally and completely changed. I ran into the Great Beast Therion at the party, and I hardly recognized him. And I discovered that I really don't like him, not at all."

"What are you saying? That I should forgive you because you've changed from indifferent to cruel?"

"No, no, no! You still don't get it!" Aleis raises the salamander to eye level. "My first thoughts as a woman went straight to Rupert. I felt, well I, I interpreted my feelings for him through the experiences of a man. I felt love for Rupert. I was in love for the first time as a woman; I didn't know what to do!"

"So that explains why you went looking for him." Py digs another beetle fragment out of his teeth. "So? Which kind of love made you involve him with the fat drunk? Your armored drugstore? Or your bloody raging tank battles?

Was it something more than your love of a good party?"

"That's not fair! I was dealing with emotions I knew nothing about. I went to Rupert, made love to him, gave him presents. But then, right away, I had this terrible feeling. I just knew I'd done something truly horrific, but I didn't know how I knew, or even what I'd done. I just felt bad. So I left, and Py, I made myself swear that I would never interfere with him again. Since Needles, you two followed your own path. I'm sorry you happened to be on my astral page, but I withdrew and left the entertainment to play itself out. I knew he couldn't get hurt too badly; I was always in control of the action to a certain extent. But now, there's a new variable—Ruby—and I've got to help him." She sets the salamander back down into her lap.

"Ruby?" Py jumps to the ground. "Who's Ruby?"

Josh stands and swipes at the back of his robe with both hands. "Allie says that Ruby got here like you; just sort of slipped onto the page by accident. She's a biker."

Py climbs Aleis's clothing, then backs himself into her bodice so that only his head and arms protrude. "Okay Allie. I'm not convinced I should forgive you, but I'll think about it. Right now, we've got to find Ru. Come on."

"Allie, Py." Josh squints into the dusk. "We may not have far to look. Isn't that a motorcycle?"

Not fifty yards away, a black clad figure astride a low bike fishtails out onto the road. As the Norton straightens, its rider leans over the handlebars and opens the throttle. The motor rages like a host of demons as Ruby passes them, heading dead on for Stonehenge. She is mostly a black blur, but they plainly see she rides alone.

As Ruby disappears into the shadows around the ring of stones, an eerie wail drifts back. "Ruuuuptuuuuuuuuuuuure!" The night, suddenly darker, smothers the sound.

-36-

Wisdom, Or Perhaps Not

Master:
Can you deny that investing a game—or any set of actions—with contrived import imbues it with unanticipated consequence?

GIL:
I deny that I care. Do whatever you will.

-37-

Do What Thou Wilt

A rustle in the dark wall of scrub oak — a careful, furtive passage — betrays the presence of some timid creature.

Rupert peers through a tight web of branches into every shadow. He strains his ears for any trace of footfall, or breath. His nose twitches as he sniffs for tell-tale odors. He looks around, then looks around again, then painfully crawls from the brush he has hidden in for the better part of the last hour. The road appears deserted; the night, complete. He pulls a thorny branch and a few dry leaves from his tangled hair, stomps his numb feet. He stretches his back, and his vertebral column snaps in a series of quick sounds, a marble running up a bone ladder. He starts walking.

The Milky Way flows directly over his head, a starry, upended river below the night sky that is the road, given depth by a canyon of dense black forest. Clean cool canyon air penetrates the accumulated fog in Rupert's brain. "Man," he says to himself, "what a day. Where the hell am I?" He walks a bit faster, and even skips for a short way.

His toe catches something solid; a metallic sound skitters across a few feet of pavement. He crouches, gropes about the darkness, raises slowly to his feet with a thin object gently cradled in both hands. He gasps and grins and dances a fancy jig. He kisses the copper flute and holds its cold metal to his cheek. "Wow! How did you get here? No matter." He blows a few monotone test notes, grins again, puts flute to lips and plays every glad song he knows. The music plummets to the firmament and runs the starry rapids, bounding from wave to wave like an ecstatic sprite riding a cork. Time itself stops to listen.

Rupert rounds a corner and is surprised to see the faint suggestion of white light leaking from around the next bend. Although his first reaction is fear for the madwoman's return, he hears nothing but his flute, and indeed, this light is too pure. Twelve bars of "Moonlight Sonata" pour unbidden from his instrument. He turns the corner into the light. The moon, full and sharp and freshly risen, rests at the bottom of a huge "V" in the mountain, a celestial olive in some colossus god's martini glass. Between the moon and Rupert there unfolds an unlikely arena. A hundred yards before him, the road ends at a circular clearing. Stonehenge glows at the center, illuminated from behind by cold moon-fire. On either side a ponderous vehicle sits: one a cartoonish dump truck; the other a sleek killing machine, an ominous harbinger of war. Rupert knows them both.

He stops playing, ducks into deep shadow. But he can detect no sign of a motorcycle; he begins again, stepping slowly and playing softly. As he nears the tank,

Rupert's spine straightens. His step grows rhythmic, martial. "The Marine Hymn" marches from his flute. He climbs onto the tank and looks down the hatch. Cooper lies in fetal curl on the upper deck.

"Hello, Cooper," Rupert chirps. "How's it going? Have you seen Py?"

"....," says Cooper. His right eyelid twitches.

"Oh, well that's okay, I'll find him. Say, what did you think of the battle back there?"

"....," says Cooper.

"I shot down two choppers," brags Rupert. "How'd you do?"

"Nute," Cooper weakly murmurs.

"No, no, he's a salamander." Rupert chuckles. "But you did see him, then?"

Cooper convulses. Both hands try to salute, collide at the bridge of his nose. "Nutes in, sir!"

"Really now, Cooper. He went into those stones?"

"Quite stoned, sir!" Cooper curls back into a ball.

"Hmmm. You didn't happen to see a huge woman dressed in leather go by here, did you?"

"....," says Cooper.

"Oh, good. Well, nice talking to you. Maybe I'll see you later." Rupert climbs down, walks the few yards to Stonehenge with a long pause between each step. He chews his lip, taps his flute against his thigh, looks over one shoulder, then the next. He squints into the interior gloom, shifts his vantage, peers again.

On the nearest stone, a paper pie plate's pyramid pupil glares at Rupert, glowing with all the freezing heat of the moon.

-38-

Table Scraps

The black cat creeps through a forest of legs: wrought-iron chair legs, elephantine oaken table legs, and a dizzying assortment of mammal legs, mostly primate. She glides with the cunning of the highly evolved huntress, avoiding some, rubbing against others, occasionally stopping to sniff and consider. Felony catches scent. She slinks through another leggy stretch of maze, then stops at a pair of bare feet, rubs against one row of scarlet toenails, crouches, and springs into Aleis's lap.

"Hello, kitty." Aleis rubs the cat's head. "Pretty Felony."

Felony purrs. She aims her golden eyes at Py.

Py sits on the table in front of Glinda, to Aleis's right. Next to Glinda, Batman sips a mint julep. He looks tired and happy. Beyond Batman: Abdul Alhazred, the good Dr. Faustus, Kate Fox, three Chinese Mandarins, Margaret Fox, an abstract representation of the dog-god Anubis, fourteen assorted mystics (Madam Blavatsky included), twenty shame-faced charlatans (Madam Blavatsky also included), the cardboard image of Joseph Smith in negative, Dan the truckin' man, Albertus Magnus, Harry, twelve winos, about twenty million incidentals, seven naked boys, a thousand and twenty one incidentals, a gigantic tin wind-up of a multiheaded dragon, the Master Therion, a few million more incidentals, the Sick Lieutenant, Joshua, and back to Aleis. Although the table is technically round, it seems as straight and true as a beam of light.

Before each guest, an elegant setting of the finest china, crystal, silver, linen. A cleverly wrapped basket of favors waits beside every aperitif glass. Graceful bouquets of dragon's wort and nettle alternate with tiny fountains of champagne and iridescent shadow.

Everyone sits side-by-side. Across the table, throughout the table's entire circumference, an odd pearly mist pulses with subtle energies.

The mist begins a steady glowing. A twice-life sized apparition of Aleis blossoms in the mist, appearing directly across from each guest. "Fellow scientists, friends, and spirits of all flavor, welcome!" She basks in a warm applause. "Thank you all for coming. I hope everyone's having as much fun as I am." A sloppy chorus of "hurrah" erupts from the twelve winos. "Before we get on with dinner, I'd just like to say that, well, this Anniversary of the Pyramids party has truly meant a lot to me, and well, just thanks again for showing up." She raises a flute of champagne. "Now a toast! To the Speed of Light! Not just a good idea, it's the Law!" A rousing refrain of "Lightspeed!" explodes from around the table with the flash of many elbows and a blaze of dopplered echo.

A sharp, pure tone pierces the echo, commands instant silence. Aleis's face no longer smiles from the mist; her image is replaced by that of a fire-eyed, darkling specter of a man. "Friends!" he calls in a thunderous voice. "Your indulgence, please! I have a toast!" Silence rules the spaces between his words.

The Master Therion, the Great Beast himself, raises a glass filled with blood-red liquor. "I propose we drink the health of the mightiest thaumaturge in the history of SOL! Our hostess, the Great She-beast, the Mistress of Mortality, the uncontested Queen of Space and Time! To our beautiful Aleis!"

Aleis covers her eyes and blushes at the deafening cheers that follow. Glinda leans forward and whispers loudly in Py's ear, "Ha! She loves it! After all, what's the good of being Queen, if nobody genuflects?"

Py watches Felony with one wary eye. "I guess it's a step up from waitress."

The first course, hearts of artichoke and truffles in a rich blood-orange marmalade, makes a grand descent from the heavens to the various place settings. The brassy fanfare is punctuated by a collective "aaaaaaah" from the guests.

The Fox sisters have each secured the ear of a Mandarin. The center Mandarin remains inscrutable. "Now there," says Kate with an impish grin, "I'll not believe you lot was *those* wise men. It strains credulity."

Kate's Mandarin nods to her sagely. "My dear Miss Fox. In the *I Ching* it is written: The heavens sag to the breaking point; it furthers one to have somewhere to go." The center Mandarin spears a truffle with a five inch fingernail, holds it to the middle of his forehead. "It is also written: Darkening of the light injures him in the left thigh. He gives aid with the strength of a horse. Who can tell?"

Second course: one perfect oyster, pulsing with life and dressed with the tiniest breath of green Japanese horseradish.

Madam Blavatsky swings back and forth between a mystic and a charlatan. She has thus far managed to confuse them both. "But surely it follows," she whines, "that if nothing can achieve the speed of light, then light itself, is the equivalent of nothing. So the absence of everything isn't vacuum, it's light. Don't you see?" Madam Blavatsky begins to dissolve into a dull gray glow.

The mystic scratches his head. The charlatan picks his nose. "That means that *darkness* is exactly the same as *everything*!" She continues to argue her point, even as she disappears completely. The mystic and the charlatan begin a discreet game of footsie.

The third course—a salad of asparagus tips and fiddlehead ferns in a dressing made from unicorn ejaculate—arrives to the accompaniment of much new Bordeaux and a crisp chamber orchestra.

Dan and Harry crowd Magnus's shoulders. Neither has been able to recognize anything placed before them as food, but they've not been completely idle. They've prematurely unwrapped their party favors. Dan and Harry each fondle a pink miniature of the Great

Pyramid of Cheops. Magnus stares at his, but refuses to touch it.

"That little thing?" Dan rolls it between two salami fingers. "Looks like dried up pig turd t'me, heh, heh."

"C'mon, old timer," Harry says, "if them doodads can turn stuff to gold, why ain't they doin' it to, like, to Danny-boy there?" He blows a steady stream of Camel smoke into the alchemist's face.

Magnus's bloodshot eyes glaze over. "You flatulent sod. As I've already explained, several times, the Stone will regain its power at midnight." He turns to Dan, lip twitching. "Will you please let me leave, now?"

"Ah, now, little buddy, you can't go until you show us how these thingers work. And you ain't had no dinner yet, anyways. Heh, heh."

The fourth course, a pan-roasted squab, glazed with orchid honey, arrives. Josh holds his squab up to the Sick Lieutenant, with both of its little wings held straight out to the side. "No, no," he's saying, "more like this."

"Wow," says the Lieutenant. "Didn't that hurt?"

"The worst of it was the hangover I had from partying the night before. Oy! And no sleep, to boot." He lays his bird back on its plate, folds its wings across its tiny breast. "So, Sickie. I've been meaning to ask. No offense now, but do you know you're only a golem?"

"Hmmmmm. Never really thought about it. Well, I guess I am, at that. A manikin, puppet, toy, doll, golem. A bloody simulacrum! Splendid! Should've seen it before!" He pulls his Meerschaum from an inside pocket, stuffs it with leftover salad, lights it.

"That doesn't bother you?" Joshua's squab stands, and begins an unsteady tap-dance.

"Why no, not in the least. In fact, dear fellow, it just occurs to me that there's a tremendous advantage!"

"Really?" Joshua kills the bird with a glance. "What?"

The Sick Lieutenant exhales an oily smoke. "If I have no will, I have no responsibility to exercise it."

The remains of the squab fly away and the fifth course drifts down to replace it. Rice balls and curried tofu are arranged with a variety of sashimi to form half-finished pentagrams.

Abdul makes the Sign of the Evil Eye and spits at his sushi. "One cannot be too careful," he tells Batman.

"Is that so?" Batman's consonants have all begun to sound like they were just fished from an angry sea. "At the very least, that should ward the sliced octopus into submission."

"You scoff! I am convinced the Elder Ones and their daemons are afoot tonight." His eyes pop even wider than their usual froggy stare; he tries to look over both shoulders simultaneously. "Listen! I hear a daemon now! They come for me!"

"Abdul, old son, get a grip." Batman lists to starboard. "That's no damned demon. That's a

Norton. This biker chick's running up and down the hallway looking for Rupert."

Abdul's teeth begin to clacker. "No, it is daemons! I know! That is the sound of Zahgurim's stomach growling! My doom is come!"

Batman laughs. "I tell you, a madwoman on a motorcycle. She almost ran me down as I came in." He nudges Glinda away from her urchin roe. "Hear that, love? Tell Abdul here what that noise is."

Glinda grips her chopsticks, leans forward, holds them two inches from the Arab's eyes, and quite seriously says, "Why, Abdul honey. Can't you tell? It's a great big fucking daemon with fangs this long."

Sixth course: mango, melon, moonfruit and marshmallows plus an assortment of cheeses served with a sparkling burgundy and thirteen centimeter silver toothpicks shaped like ceremonial daggers.

Aleis chews a piece of moonfruit and draws runes in a soft cheese with the tip of a little dagger. She has eaten quietly, seemingly absorbed in whatever entertainments played out in the mists across the table. She looks pensive, not lonely or bored. Currently, she watches a slapstick scene staged at the Beast Brothers. An efficiently busy Philomela has just filled a cowboy's ten gallon hat with twelve gallons of chili. She moves to the next customer without breaking rhythm. Aleis sighs, and the scene disappears. She swallows without savor.

Py watches Felony; Felony watches Py.

Aleister prods at a chunk of mango without interest. "Py? What do you suppose has happened to Rupert? You don't suppose he could've wandered off the page do you? I'd hate to think he's gotten lost in the real world."

"Who knows? He's probably better off without either of us, anyway." He yanks a silver dagger from a stone-shaped lump of Camembert, shows it to the cat, places it within easy reach. "So, as long as we're talking, tell me about Philomela. How does she fit into all this?"

"The solid gold bar wench. Philomela's an astral double of Felicity, at her oldest state. Just another toy."

Py lets one eye make contact with Aleis. The other remains vigilant. "What became of the real Felicity?"

"She's been dead for over seven hundred years." She pushes away her plate, trades the glass of burgundy for a martini. "Py, when I animated the statue, I didn't do any better than you did with Rupert. When I brought the body to life, I gave it a new soul. I guess there's no way around that. Real bodies have souls. Maybe it's all just a function of brain chemistry."

Py almost gets angry, shakes his head instead. "Tell me you didn't destroy a viable soul so that you could live."

Instead of defensive, she just looks beaten. "No. No matter what you think of me, I could never do a thing like that. Maybe I could have once.... No. The new soul is still in her real body."

"She's still alive?"

Aleis takes the piece of mango after all, dips it in gin, pops it in her mouth. "Of course, of course. Her name is Felicia. She lives in Oregon, just off the page." She licks mango juice from her lower lip. "You'll get to see her in minute; she's the grand finale."

Py throws her an incredibly nasty look, both eyes. She laughs for the first time in hours. "Oh Py! She chose to dance for us of her own free will! Honest, she begged me for the chance! It's what she does."

The salamander has just gone back to watching the cat when an icy thought ripples through him. "Allie." Forgetting the danger completely, he walks closer, places his tiny orange hand on hers. "If the new soul's still in its original body," he says, with more sympathy than outrage, "*what the hell are you*?"

Felony purrs, and cleans her claws.

Dessert is an Italian ice made from the glacier atop Mount Olympus, subtly flavored with wormwood and backed by Pernod and strong coffee.

The Master Therion sips cognac and felates an enormous cigar. He takes a watch from his vest, glances at it, replaces it.

Aleis reappears in the mist across the table. "Ladies and gentlemen and whatever else. You've all enjoyed the meal, I trust? Well, I only interrupt to introduce our last act. We are about to experience the rare pleasure of a truly magnificent exotic dancer. As you will see, her talent is exceeded only by her beauty." Her brows knit slightly; she pinches her lower lip. "Enough talk. Friends, I give you the one and only Felicia!"

The light dims, the crowd quiets. The Master leans back in his seat and smokes.

Felicia stands in the middle of an old hardwood stage, lit from offstage and below by rich golden spots. She wears the home-spun simplicity of a Thirteenth Century serving girl with charm and panache. She courtesies. An electric hush settles into the ballroom as the first notes of Tchaikovsky's 1812 Overture begin to build. Felicia's hips describe tiny circles, alternating left, right. Her arms create shadow forms in the space about her head. She takes the hem of her skirt in one hand and floats it like it had no more substance than the wind, twirls it in delicate spider silk patterns, teases it into current and wave. Uneven snapshots of cream white leg hold to the eye well past the event of their exposure. The music turns French; Felicia responds with bold abandon. One movement, too swift to follow, and a perfectly formed breast leaps from its sheath in a gentle arc. She spins on the ball of one foot, with dizzying speed. Her skirt takes flight, sails about her hips, then detaches and is gone. A tiny golden g-string hugs to the valleys in the muscles of her legs; a puff of dark blond hair peeks over the top. The Overture pounds and thunders. Felicia twirls out of her peasant blouse. Her right breast looks very like the left. She rolls her belly, the g-string falls apart and drops to the stage.

The Master looks again at his watch. He stands, blows a kiss in the general direction of Aleis, and leaves.

Felicia walks the length of the stage on her hands with her strong legs in full splits. She completes a slow rotation as the music roars. Church bells ring of victory and the cannonade begins. The air above the banquet explodes with fireworks.

With everyone else's attention riveted, Harry creeps among the guests, stealing their baskets of favors. He fills a huge sack, improvised from Dan's multicolored tee shirt.

Felicia's body bows backwards and she falls into a bridge. She pulls herself to her feet using the muscles of her legs alone, and everyone but Harry gasps in unison. Even Dan is moved. With every cannon shot, hundreds of fiery blossoms bloom. She sticks a small, cleverly designed roman candle to each nipple and lights them. Fountains of sparks spew onto the stage.

Py has let the fireworks distract him. Felony springs. They tussle about the table, knocking over glasses and bouquets. Py manages to get his dagger into play, and using it as a lever breaks free and leaps from the table.

He tries to run with the dagger in hand, but soon abandons the weapon and scuttles away on four feet. The cat follows in an evil slink, the very tip of her tail lashing like a scorpion's sting.

Dan hauls himself to his fat feet and waddles toward the exit. His bare paunch quivers and undulates in time with the music. "Harry, you dumb bastard! C'mon buddy, we got enough!"

Harry grabs a few more baskets and sprints for the door. "I'm a comin' Danny boy!"

The cresting coda ignites a furious explosion of colored light, fire, smoke and thunder. Aleis leans behind Joshua and taps the Sick Lieutenant on the arm. "Sickie, come with me. We've got to find Rupert. I just figured something out! My feelings for the boy! That son of a bitch is my goddamned son!!"

The last cannon shot echoes away, the last of the fireworks sparkles into darkness. Felicia bows low, with a sweeping gesture. She gasps for air through a broad grin. And Tchaikovsky, the dead old faggot, has a wet dream in his grave.

-39-
Meat Parts III: The Final Conflict

Hollow booms and sharp pops fill the night sky with all the colors of fire, challenging the moon's cold glare with pastel shadows. In the changing light from above, Stonehenge is a dancing, gaptoothed grin. In the deepest shade of the stones, strange business is afoot.

"It's about time," says Harry, "for the damn things to work. Twelve, straight up." His face glows red, lit by the glowing stump of a Camel. "Yep, twelve."

"O-boy," says Dan. "Well, dump a couple of 'em in the back with the meat. Just don't touch 'em, heh, heh. Then again, even a skinny runt like you'd make enough gold t' be worth melting down. Heh." He opens a pint with chocolate-stained teeth, drains half. He stands on the dumper's running boards, watches Harry climb up.

Harry gingerly shakes three pyramids out of the bag. They land, right-sides-up, in the open mouth of a pig's head. At first, nothing. The two caricatures hold their buffoonish breaths. A searing golden light burnishes the sky; Dan and Harry duck. They raise their heads, and gasp in unison. The pig's head, two empty pint bottles, and several random pieces of offal have been transmuted. Harry picks up a golden hoof with two fingers. "Heavy enough," he says. An unidentifiable bovine fragment begins to glow. "Feels about right." His jaw slacks and the cigarette falls unnoticed, instantly changes to gold. "Goddammit, Danny, we done it! We're rich!" He howls like a jackal. The spinal column of a goat lights up with a flash.

Dan quivers and shakes as he heaves his mass into the cab. "C'mon, Harry. Throw the rest of them py-ram-id thingers back there. Let's get the hell out a' here!" He fires up the truck, jams it into reverse and manages to back it up no more than twenty feet before the growing weight of golden meat parts adds up enough to blow all eight rear tires simultaneously. The combined explosion is louder by far than any skyrocket.

"Standing by to return fire, sir." Cooper's voice rattles, a dead sound. "Target at 12:00 and steady, sir. Target lock positive, sir, five by five." His eyes track randomly. "Range twenty meters, sir. Obstructions at ten and two, clear line of fire. Warhead armed and ready, sir."

"Well met, soldier." The Master Therion lays a gloved hand on Cooper's shoulder. "You may fire at will."

-40-

Fallout

Rupert edges around the stone, all senses twitching in concert, and finds himself in an endless hallway. He leans back hard against the door jam, blinks deliberately, rubs at his eyes with gritty knuckles. The hall remains endless. Across from him, distant whistles and pops and subtle flashes of colored light leak through a marble arch. He takes one tiny step away from the door, holding on with one hand as if reluctant to break some critical contact. He looks both ways, blinks again, takes another half-step. "Hello?" His voice cracks along with the fireworks. "Hello? Anybody home?" A stirring crescendo echoes faintly through the arch, and with it, the curious blended scents of cordite and marijuana. He releases his grip on the door.

An orange blur zips through the arch, skids sideways across the floor, gallops and scrabbles and flops and spins, smacks around Rupert's ankle like a damp towel.

"Py!" shouts Rupert.

"Ru!" shouts Py.

Rupert drops to his haunches, cradles the salamander in both hands. "Where've you been, you silly orange lizard?"

"It's nice to see you again, too, Ru." Py blows a sloppy raspberry at Felony, who skulks back and forth in front of the arch with a frustrated series of meows.

"Where is everybody? The Marines, Aleis...."

"They're all around here someplace." Py climbs Rupert's arms, scales his hair, settles into a perch on his shoulder. "Listen, kid, it's time. It's time you learned a few things. About your life, and me, and Aleis." Above the fading sound of fireworks, a throaty drone warbles. Py cocks his head.

"About Allie?" A chill dread starts at the base of his spine, races the length of it, ends in hackles. "Time I learn about what?"

"Not here. This is important." The droning drops in pitch, gains in volume. "Let's go somewhere and sit." Py squints down the hall.

Rupert takes a full-sized step toward the party.

The salamander reins him in with two hands full of hair. "Oh my Gods!" He hisses into Rupert's ear. "It's Ruby."

The original chill dread gathers up all of the color in Rupert's face and with it flees back toward his tailbone in full panic retreat. At the same time, he sees her — leaning over the handlebars and growing larger by the second, breasts exposed and hair trailing, a mutant cross between Valkerie and comet. Rupert hesitates, stuck like a bug to a bumper, a deer in the headlights, a lump in the throat. Py slaps his ear, hard. He half-turns, stumbles. Sees Ruby lean out to the side, arm extended, so close he can see one nipple is slightly larger, slightly redder, than the other. Time turns to syrup, each nanosecond dripping in torment. Her hand flexes, her forearm tenses for the impact of the catch.

Py bites down on Rupert's ear, hard enough to draw blood. "Run, you stupid asshole, RUN!!!"

Rupert yelps, tucks the salamander under his arm like a football and dives headfirst through the nearest doorway. He does not look back. Does not chance to see the pulse of actinic light, the sparkling geyser, the prismatic mushroom.

From behind, he hears the rapidly diminishing echo of a painful wail, "Ruuuuuupptuuuuuuuure!   I   fucking looooooove you!"

He hits soft ground and somersaults; he rolls over wet spongy grass, free and safe, until his head abruptly connects with something as hard as a stump; sparks of light play out inside his throbbing skull.

Darkness.

-41-

Anchors A'weigh!

Aleis and the Sick Lieutenant stand at the edge of a large clearing. In the center, a black circle smolders. The clearing is completely empty, save for moonlight and a smoky haze.

"Oh-oh," says Aleis.

"But what's all this..." He waves his feathered cap at the grim tableau. "What's happened? Where's Stonehenge gotten off to? Where's my bloody tank?"

She lights a cigarette and sighs. "Want my guess? One of Cooper's nutes went off."

"I didn't hear anything. And why aren't we dead?"

"Well, this is only conjecture, you understand." She paces and smokes. "He must've fired it into the hall. Everything within and around the stone circle got vaporized and all the debris—tank, truck, stones, even the sounds—got sucked up with the remains of my poor party." She sniffs the air. "Might still be some fallout, though. We better get off this page. It'll all settle here."

"Oh my Gods." The Lieutenant pulls Aleis into his arms, holds her face between his hands, tries to find a spark of the horror that he feels in Aleis's eyes. "It was the anchor! Without the anchor, what happened to the party?"

"It's gone, of course. And going fast."

He sputters, unbelieving. "All those people...."

"Really, Sickie." Aleis suddenly grins. "No serious harm done." She kisses him, takes his arm, starts walking. "Everyone there was either spirit or puppet. The spirits will have the grandest adventure in millennia, but they'll eventually find their way back to their own universes. Maybe in time for the next Anniversary! And as to the puppets, well, you're the only one I really liked, anyway."

Only somewhat mollified, the Lieutenant scrapes out his pipe as they walk. "What ever possessed you? I mean, you say you created all this—what on Earth were you thinking? Neutron bombs? Surely you had a reason."

She rolls her cigarette butt between the palms of her hands. It gets smaller and smaller and finally, disappears. "You know? For the life of me. I cannot remember." She leans into him, puts both arms around his trim waist. "I do sort of wonder, though...."

They reach a place where the road joins a major highway. There is a slight ripple in the air along the boundary, and the breeze makes a sound like ruffling paper. A fine old automobile waits, parked on the grass just off the road. Something stands in the middle of the road, right at the join. It is Rupert's slender ash walking stick, balanced on end. It casts an indigo moon shadow, pointed the same direction as the highway, the same direction as the car.

Aleis takes it in her hand. A single tear falls. The head of the stick is carved in the stern likeness of the Master Therion. "Goddamn myself," she whispers, and flings the infernal relic as far from herself as she can.

-42-

No Harm

A fine rain gathers in cool pools on Rupert's eyes. The pools brim and water runs down his cheeks: cheap tears. The tiny streams bend across his cheekbones and follow their natural drainage into his ears. Cool fresh water tarries for a second, then dribbles out to splash against already saturated moss. The air pulsates with rainsong, life, mist, and the aroma of wet pine. Rupert opens his eyes, wipes them on a bare arm, drags himself to his elbows. He shakes his bruised head slowly, and droplets spray in every direction. He groans. Head tilted back, he opens his mouth to the sky. He sits up.

"Welcome back." Py floats on his back in a rotten stump full of water. "How do you feel?" He backstrokes in lazy circles.

"Oh my head...." Rupert stands, takes a moment to balance, walks to the center of the glade, to the large charred area there. He stoops and lays his right palm flat on the black surface. Steam rises ghostly from the char. "I smell Oregon. Mildew and decay."

"Entropy," says Py. "This is Oregon. And entropy always wins." He snaps up an undercautious caterpillar, sighs, and climbs out of the pool. "Ru."

Rupert doesn't move. "It's so pointless. The universe is random. I don't understand anything." He plows his hand through a soaked rat's nest of hair, leaving a dark gray streak against the rust.

The salamander makes a tiny orange fist. "Ru. Listen to me. You've been jacked around long enough. It's time for you to learn some unpleasant truths."

A faint pearly glow bleeds into the eastern sky.

"I mean," continues Rupert, "I feel like I have no control over my life. Things just happen to me. Weird things. Things that seem to have no meaning, no purpose—no cause, only effect. Weird effects." He kicks at the burnt earth. "I feel like I'm living in a dream. Somebody else's dream."

An owl hoots into the pattering rain.

Rupert walks the circumference of the black circle, arms out like a tightrope artist. "Colorado Springs," he chants, "is full of slimy things." He watches the ground. When he completes the circle, Py is there waiting. Rupert sits cross-legged next him. "There are some car tracks over there. We can follow them to a road, and thumb the hell away from here. Go someplace, anyplace. Settle down for awhile, I guess. Maybe I'll see Aleis again, someday."

"Sure, Ru. We'll go. But first, I've got to tell you some things. Some things about Aleis, and well, about us." Py clears his tiny throat. "It's time you learned about your parents."

-43-

Varnish

An inchoate ash settles uniformly over the page. It is radioactive and contains a variety of strange particles. There are atoms that once belonged to great mysterious stones. There are atoms of earth, air, fire, water. There are atoms of carbon steel that once were armor. There are atoms that belonged to life and atoms that belonged to death. There are atoms that were Harry and twice as many atoms that were Dan. Atoms of Cooper, atoms of gold, pink Philosopher's atoms all settle together in a single cloud of dust, settle evenly onto every surface.

Even in this dilute state the Philosopher Stone maintains some power. A fine golden ash covers all. The page is gilt.

-44-

The Last Limerick

The painter's outstretched ocher hands
Create a dream of pastel lands
     Where brush is tree,
     And palette sea,
And waves of paint sculpt canvas sands.

-45-

The Spice of Life

Time is morning. The obscure sun swims a thick gray sky. Cold rain drizzles through the air, clings to every surface. A brisk rivulet runs along both sides of a twisted narrow road. A thin silvery light filters through cloud and tree to leave vague shadows the color of tarnished coin. Rising mist twines with the odor of soft decay.

Rupert plods the center of the road, hands jammed in pockets, eyes glued to the pavement no further than the next step away. Goosepimples and sodden wrinkles cover every square inch of skin like palette knife textures. His clothes cover him like a coat of wet acrylic. Red hair hangs dripping like a bundle of saturated fox-tail brushes. With every step, his shoes fart and gurgle like tubes of paint getting over a few air bubbles.

Py rides a soggy shoulder, grinning. His orange hide glistens and sparkles, nearly glows. He talks in low tones to Rupert's ear. "...So naturally you're confused. I mean, you are definitely a real human being, it's just that, well, you're a little *contrived*. To your credit I must say that you've developed into a fair approximation of a man, for a man born without a childhood." Between words, the salamander licks rain drops from it bulging eyes.

A shiver starts in Rupert's knees, vibrates the length of his body, ends in a chattering of teeth. He clenches his jaws tight and hugs himself.

"You want to know what really pisses me off, Ru? I'll tell you. It's the way that bitch played party games with your emotions. Like, she knew you never had a chance to acculturate, or learn how to deal with sex or love or any of that stuff. She just coldly decides to fuck you, just to see what would happen. And Jesus, technically, you're her son!"

At the word "coldly," Rupert shudders again. "Get off it," he mumbles. "If she's my mother, then you're my damned father."

"Has it been so awful? Come on now. It's not like I haven't tried. I mean, what should I know about raising people? I'm just a sprite, after all. Don't you think I've at least tried?"

"Yeah, you did what you could; I'm grateful. But hell, I'm soaked and freezing my ass off; I don't know where the fuck I'm going; I don't know where the fuck I've been; my head hurts; I just found out that my mommy's a transsexual witch and daddy's a frog; I'm sore and depressed and tired and hungry.... Just don't talk about Aleis that way. Okay?"

"Sure, okay Ru. Whatever you say." Py rolls his eyes in opposite directions. "So I'm a frog, now. Sheesh." They walk an endless while in silence and nothing really changes, except the worthless sun swims higher.

Py first spots the tavern, a rustic timbered building squatting in the midst of a gravel clearing, just back from the road. A neon sign splashes blue and violet light across two parked cars. "Ru! Civilization!"

Rupert looks up. Buzzing blue light spells out "The Spice of Life," and below that, in violet: "A Quality Burlesque Establishment." He lets fly a wild whoop and assays a stiff legged jog. He splashes through puddles, rounds a guard rail, bounces off both cars, and slams hard against the door. It opens the width of a number six brush.

Warm light and friendly music rush out to greet him.

-46-

The End of Wisdom

Master:
So, then. Gameplay can be seen as an effort to control, by will alone, the circumstances which surround chaotic events, without affecting their inherent randomness.

GIL:
Sounds to me like you're trying to take credit for an extremely lucky outcome. Another game, double or nothing?

Master:
As Ye do no harm, do what Thou wilt shall be the whole of the Law. Love is the Law. Love under will.

-47-

The Whole of the Law

Rupert sits at the bar. A borrowed robe hugs his shoulders, squeezes his chest, caresses his forearms. It is far too small, and far too reminiscent of a fluff-dried flamingo, but it is dry, warm, and smells like a woman. His own clothes stretch on the hearth before a gay fire; his shoes hang by their laces from the mantle. Rupert sold his flute to the bartender for the price of a grilled cheese sandwich and a few hot toddies. He sips his third toddy while the bartender removes an empty plate.

"Never heard of anybody keeping a salamander pet before," says the bartender. "They easy to housebreak?"

"Wouldn't know." Rupert licks buttery crumbs from his moustache. "Py housebroke me. Nice place. Do much business?"

"Enough. It's early yet, that's why no one's here. Dancer'll get here pretty soon; you'll like her. Best damned stripper in the whole rain forest." He cuts limes and wipes glasses and straightens bottles while he talks. His hands work on their own initiative.

A gust of damp air follows Felicia through the door. "Hey, Eddie," she says to the bartender, "look what I found out back on the dumpster. A big orange newt!" She sets Py on the bar, sees Rupert in all his pink flummery, raises one eyebrow, turns back to Eddie. She hands him her coat and umbrella. "Never seen one so big, have you?"

Py waddles down the bar towards Rupert.

"That's no newt," says Eddie. "That's this here gentleman's pet salamander. Name of Py— the amphibian, not the gentleman. What was your name again, bud? This is my favorite girl in the whole wild world, Felicia."

"Rupert." A blush two shades darker than the robe feathers his cheeks. "Maybe my clothes are dry." He points with both hands, levers off the stool onto cold hardwood, hops from bare foot to bare foot. "Uh, better get myself dressed." He scoops up his jeans and tee shirt, heads for the men's room.

Py lays flat on his stomach in front of the girl, staring with both eyes. He scratches the back of his head with a back foot.

"Hey, Eddie." Felicia bounces onto a narrow stage. "I worked up a couple of new moves. Wanna see? Play something nasty, you know, like sex or lust."

Eddie comes around the bar to the jukebox, punches a number. A bluesy grind exudes from hidden places among the rafters. The stripper smiles, closes her eyes, begins to dance. Eddie wipes his hands on his apron, folds his arms, watches with professional interest.

Rupert exits the restroom with the pink robe draped over his arm. The pit of his stomach freezes, his jaw drops dead, the robe flutters to the floor. The rusted wheels in his brain begin to turn. He watches with fascination as Felicia removes her shirt. His eyes pulse to the beat. He struggles to form a coherent thought.

The girl wears metallic pasties with foot-long braided silver tassels. She dips at the knees, and when she rises, the tassels whip into action, spinning in opposite directions in time to the slow beat.

Eddie claps along with the rhythm. The frontal lobes of Rupert's brain spin with opposite rotation; his knees knock out a spastic syncopation.

Py watches Felicia with an altogether different sort of interest. He mumbles rhetorical questions to himself and scratches his head, and draws arcane diagrams on the bar with a moistened finger. "If Allie really created this whole mess, why does she first appear on the entertainment page? And if she really didn't bring Ru and me onto it…. And what about that spooky DeSoto? Wait a minute. Philomela is supposedly a simulacrum without a soul." He sketches:

Rupert = manufactured body + new soul

Felicia = reconstituted body + manufactured soul

Aleis = old soul + new.... *New what?*

He circles "What."

"What the hell is Allie? Hmmm. Didn't she say that maybe all bodies get souls? Not possible. Wouldn't Allie, I mean Aleister, know that? Not every manufactured body gets a soul. Dan and Harry, now there's a couple of poster boys for soulless. Batman? I think not. Too one-dimensional. But what's the difference between Philomela, Felicia, and Aleis? They look a lot alike, like…" He pauses. His eyes bulge, more than usual. "…one woman at three different ages. BUT—and it's a big one—how can one being from three different times co-exist in the same place? Answer: THEY CANNOT. By all the gods! That's it!" He wets a finger in Rupert's drink and writes: SOL. "Damn! It's about Time!" Py rolls from the bar and lands with a loud splat. "It's a big enough plot hole to drive a DeSoto through! Philomela and Felicia are *characters* in a play created by Aleis who herself is a *character* in a story created by the Master who is a *character* in a painting created by an Elder Demon who is a *character* in a book written by *some ridiculous sonofabitch author for the amusement of Who the Fuck Cares!* It doesn't matter; we're in a goddamn *novel!*" He beelines for Rupert's leg.

Felicia's tassels cut a lemniscate in the air.

"Ru!" He hits Rupert's leg at top speed, doesn't slow until he has a double handful of red hair. "Ru, listen. I had it all wrong. Everything's working out fine! Well, as fine as this absurd plot will permit. Anything bad I may have said about Allie, I hereby eat. Raw. With sincere apologies. She couldn't have done anything to intentionally hurt you! Damn I wish I hadn't said those things to her. No, really Ru. Aleis is innocent. Of all charges." He laughs, the sound of a salamander barking. "Everything's working out just fine. Be sure to make nice with Felicia; I think you are going to get along famously. You two will make a charming denouement." He lets go of Rupert's hair, slides down his arm to sit in the crook of his elbow. "Hey, Rupert. Um, my job here is over, I guess. I have to go back to GIL, now. I can feel him pulling.... It's been real fun. I'm going to miss you, kid." He blinks six times. "Be good."

Felicia cracks both tassels with the sharp report of cannons.

"Do what you will, Rupert, shall be the whole of the Law. There's more I didn't tell you. Love is the Law. Love under Will. Goodbye, son. Goodbye, man."

The song rises into the rafters, vanishes from whence it came. She makes an exaggerated bow to Eddie, who applauds with vigor. Rupert finally looks at Py.

"Sorry, what did you say?" But Py's eyes have lost their spark and track randomly. The salamander shies away from Rupert's touch, thrashes about, falls to the floor, and drags itself like an amphibian to a dark corner. It curls up to sleep.

Rupert follows for a few steps. One eyebrow wrinkles. "Py?"

"Rupert," Felicia says, "hand me my robe, okay?"

He turns from the salamander back to the stripper. "Sure, here." He picks the robe up and hands it over. "I hope you don't mind my using it. I was drenched."

"Not at all, sweetie. 'Though I hope it looks better on me. Can I buy you a drink? If I do, you'll have to come talk to me. Deal?"

Rupert grins and stuffs his hands into his pockets. "Sure, it's a deal." He slides into a candle-lit booth; she slips in next to him. "You know, I could swear I know you from somewhere."

She laughs, a song of lyres. "I was about to ask you the same thing."

Rupert's eyes shine opalescent luminosity. "Ever been to Colorado Springs?"

Outside the clouds have rent, and old Sol smiles down at a clean and sparkling world.

-48-

Gesso

Step back and look. It is finished. The lacquer has dried to give the page a golden tint. The colors beneath, predominately rust and ocher and deep blue-violet, are set. The concept and design combine elements of shade over light to present a remarkable illusion of depth. It is a fairly nice attempt, but it is far from perfect. There are flaws. A tiny round burn hole mars one corner, perhaps a dropped cigarette ash or a burning marijuana seed. A subtle distortion of perspective creates an indescribable nausea. The lacquer's tint, a bit too thick, drains life away from the gentler shadings. The page, while a work of some promise, is somewhat overdone. But not a waste. Lessons have been learned, craft polished, themes presented and played about. Time well spent.

An opaque spray descends across the page, covers it smoothly and evenly and completely with white. The page is blank. Born again. Virgin.

-49-

Love Is the Law

"Here, Kitty," Aleis says. She puts her hands on her knees, makes a soft clucking sound. "Here Felony, here baby." The black cat appears, as if from nowhere, and jumps into her arms purring.

The Sick Lieutenant holds the old DeSoto's door. He has traded his uniform for a lavender tuxedo, complete with top hat, tails and cane. "What a marvelous car," he says.

"Would you care to drive, Sickie, dear?"

"Would I? I'd love to!" He waits for Aleis to slide in, then follows. He caresses the steering wheel, makes love to the instrument panel with his eyes.

Aleis hugs the cat to her breast for a moment, then settles it at her feet and begins assembling two martinis.

The Lieutenant starts the car; it purrs like a cat. "You know, the only thing that bothers me is this soul business. If every time a body gets created, it has a soul, doesn't that imply that the concept of 'soul' really refers to basic biochemical neurology? And doesn't that mean I've got one, too?"

She hands him a drink, slides over lasciviously. "Why, Sickie, dear! You're beginning to sound like a true scientist!" She runs one hand along his leg. "The real question, of course, is: Who cares? As long as we have will, we can love. And as long as we can love...." She pets the cat with one bare foot. "...we got all the soul we need."

He bites his lip. "That's just the thing. How do I know if I've got will?"

"Damned if I can tell you. Does the cat have will? The car? Do I?" She nestles into his side. "So, where shall we go?"

"Hmmmm." He shifts into reverse. "How about East?"

"Fine with me," Aleis says. She sucks the pimento from an olive. "I just need to get away from here, go someplace where everybody just does whatever the hell they want. I'm still depressed about Rupert. You don't suppose he escaped the neutron bomb, do you?"

"No way," says the Sick Lieutenant. "He's atoms. Shit. Outa'. Luck."

Aleis sighs. "You're probably right. Say, you ever been to Colorado Springs?"

The old DeSoto turns east, into the faintest sketch of a new dawn. An irresistible grin lights the way.

— end —